Does a Boy Get a Chance to Work on a Fort Every Day?

Tom gave Ben the wood plane with great reluctance, and while Ben began to sharpen board after board, Tom sat on an empty barrel in the shade, dangling his legs, munching on the first of many promised apples, every now and then surveying the landscape to make sure there was no imminent Zum attack. Although the undead were not in attendance, other boys happened by. By the time Ben was fagged out, Tom had traded the next chance to Billy Fisher for a kite, in good repair. And when he was played out, Johnny Miller bought in with the scrap of what was said to be a Zum shirt, covered with holes from many bullets and no little amount of blood. And so on and so on, hour after hour. By the end of the afternoon, Tom was literally rolling in a kind of wealth. Besides the treasures already mentioned, he had twelve marbles, a variety of startlingly white Zum teeth raked out of a pyre, . . . the last edition of a one-page newspaper from a small town nearby entirely burned and razed by the Zum, a tin soldier, a brass doorknob, the handle of a broken knife, several prayer cards of people killed in earlier attacks, and a handful of firecrackers.

THE ADVENTURES OF
TOM SAWYER
AND THE
UNDEAD

MARK TWAIN
AND
DON BORCHERT

TOR®

A Tom Doherty Associates Book · New York

This is a work of fiction. All the characters, organizations, and events portrayed in this novel are either products of the author's imagination or are used fictitiously.

THE ADVENTURES OF TOM SAWYER AND THE UNDEAD

Copyright © 2010 by Don Borchert

All rights reserved.

A Tor Book
Published by Tom Doherty Associates, LLC
175 Fifth Avenue
New York, NY 10010

www.tor-forge.com

Tor® is a registered trademark of Tom Doherty Associates, LLC.

ISBN 978-0-7653-6663-4

First Edition: August 2010
First Mass Market Edition: September 2011

Printed in the United States of America

0 9 8 7 6 5 4 3 2 1

To Bob Borchert, who neither came nor departed
with the appearance of Halley's Comet. He departed
watching an NCAA semifinals basketball game,
an unfinished word jumble on his lap.

To Sally and Andrea and Beth and Rosie.

To Bob and Donna Perkins.

To Ian, John, and Ryan—
oh my, what a bunch. Big tough ones.

To Theresa, Curtis, and Rhea,
constant supporters from within the library.

To Greg Bobulinski,
jazz trumpet player extraordinaire,
who reminds us that life is not merely endless commerce.

To Lynne Wolverton.

ACKNOWLEDGMENTS

To Andrea, who gave me the idea with a straight face.

To my agent, Melissa Flashman, and her assistant, Alex Friedstein—the spurious foreword was his idea, and I absolutely owe him a beer or two. Very nice. Shows a devious mind.

To copyeditor Christina MacDonald, who tried to make me look more literate than I am.

To Mark Twain. I can only say what I used to tell my parents when I did something horrible and could not talk myself out of it—I'm sorry, and I'll never do it again.

EDITOR'S NOTE

In the 1870s, at the time of its original publication, *The Adventures of Tom Sawyer and the Undead* served as a rallying cry to both the global literary community and laymen alike. Up until this point Mark Twain had made his mark primarily as a journalist and a humorist. Essays and short stories were his stock-in-trade. With the introduction of the Zum virus (eventually traced to a strain of alphaherpesvirinae in the 1920s), everything changed. The virus cast its pall on the arts and literature. In correspondence with lifelong friend and fellow writer William D. Howells, Twain complained that the constant, random threat of Zum violence was like "trying to write a love sonnet wrapped in a foul horse blanket. Stultifying and uncomfortable, by the time you are halfway through, the stink has crept its way onto the page!"* For Twain and Borchert, the former town librarian who supplemented his income as a reporter, the devastation caused by the sudden foundering of the *Hannibal Post-Courier*—the newspaper at which they had both

* *The Correspondence of Samuel L. Clemens and William D. Howells,* 1872–1910, Harvard University Press, 1962.

apprenticed—was the last straw. They resolved to form a writing partnership and fight back.

In an angry polemic that was originally printed in the *Hannibal Daily Clarion* (the only remaining newspaper in Hannibal) and eventually reprinted in *The New York Times*, Twain wrote:

> The children still play the games they have always played, the same sun still rises in the morning, and one season still drifts into the next, but the adults all seem to be wasting away. They've conceded defeat. I walk down the street and everyone seems pallid, drawn, pinched with worry, everyone is putting an extra lock on the door, stocking up on cartridges and potable water, bracing for the end of the world. I for one—and Borchert too—have had it! It was the end of *that* world, and good riddance to it. Let it sink beneath the waves. It is time to conjure up a new world, to take a step forward!*

It was the right time for such a statement. Newspapers across the country reprinted the letter, and in areas that were now without newspapers, the letter was printed and distributed at churches and other public meeting places.

Arguably their most popular, if not most critically acclaimed book, *The Adventures of Tom Sawyer and the Undead* struck an immediate, sensational chord around the world. This was particularly true in countries where Zum

* My Impressions of The Age of Zum, 1900.

infestation, in combination with rapid urbanization and industrialization, were introducing a period of great societal transformation. It was clear we had reached the dawn of a brave new epoch. The duo found themselves sought out as experts on Zum containment and palliative remedies. Rudyard Kipling, who was in India during the initial Zum outbreak, met Twain and Borchert in 1889 and credited them both with his continuation as a writer, a profession he nearly abandoned in his zeal to rid the world of the Zum. During this encounter, Borchert and Twain presented him with a Missouri meerschaum pipe to commemorate the occasion, with a note indicating the gift was intended for the great author Kipling, not the adventurer. Several years later, Kipling dedicated his poem "Soldier, Soldier" to the writing team.

In their later years, the writers grew more and more pessimistic over the prospect of a realistic victory over the Zum plague. Following the death and subsequent decapitation of Twain's beloved wife during a Zum intrusion in 1890, their novels took a dark and cynical turn, which bore influence on their later work *The Resurrection of Pudd'nhead Wilson* and *A Yank in the Time of King Arthur*. Soon after, they ended their collaboration and Twain began writing with a new partner, Bret Harte, but this collaboration was acrimonious and short-lived.

Twain was honored by Yale University in 1901 with two honorary degrees, in both arts and medicine. He moved to the Baja Peninsula where he wrote his last works on efforts there to become the fifty-sixth state. He died on April 21,

1910, only twenty years before the first successful Zum vaccine was developed. Borchert accompanied popular writer Ambrose Bierce into Mexico to get a firsthand look at that country's revolution, and was declared dead in 1913 after a lengthy search.

J. Clement Seagrave, Ph.D.
Professor of Comparative Literature
Middlebrook College
Columbus, Ohio

The Adventures of
TOM SAWYER
and the
UNDEAD

1

Aunt Polly on Alert

The old woman gripped the even older hickory axe handle and held her breath for a moment in an attempt to improve her hearing. The axe handle by itself wasn't going to do her much good, but the only gun in the house was behind the door in the drawing room, too far away. The axe handle would have to do, and if an opportunity presented itself, she'd make her way to the gun.

"Tom!"

No answer.

"Tom!"

No answer.

It was just like him to be playing and not mindful of what was going on in the world around him, and usually there was no harm in that—in acting like a boy, in the summer. But the house wasn't in the village proper, and that was worrisome. The Zum didn't have much luck in town—any town—and so a lot of people who were nervous living out by themselves moved back to luxuriate in the warmth and security of having a great many neighbors. The old woman was not like that. She had lived in the house for too long, a lifetime, and it was a home to her. Twenty, even ten years ago, one of the Zum would have been no match for her. Now she wasn't so sure, but she wasn't about to be moved out of her own home by fear in any case.

"Tom!"

Still no answer.

The old woman pulled her spectacles down and looked about the room. It was darker in the room than was normal for the middle of the day, but the house had been mostly boarded up for a while now—at least on the first floor. It seemed the Zum had never mastered the skill of clambering up the trellises and drainpipes and so had never gotten in the habit of dropping unannounced into second-floor bed-rooms, which was a comfort, if only a small one. They could still rampage through the first floor if you decided to hole up in a second-floor bedroom, and many times they'd start a fire and wait for you to drop out of the sky like ripe fruit. The people in the know said the Zum weren't that smart and that it was an unintentional misfortune when this hap-pened, but no one ever made a proper study of it.

Aunt Polly looked perplexed for a moment, and then she said in a voice loud enough for the furniture to hear:

"Well, if I get my hands on you, I'll—"

She did not finish, for by this time she was on her knees,

peering under furniture and punching underneath the bed with the axe handle, and she needed all her strength for this activity. She found nothing but a cat who scrambled out and hid somewhere else.

"I never did see the beat of that boy."

She took off her shoes and walked quietly to the open front door and looked out into what passed for her summer garden. The tomatoes and squash plants were unattended, overgrown with jimpson weed, but untrammeled. This in itself was a good sign that the Zum were not about, as they were oblivious to lanes and walkways, and were easy to spot by the disorder of their wake. She unbuttoned the top button at her throat and lifted her voice as if in church on Christmas Eve:

"You-u-u. Tom!"

The floorboards creaked behind her and she whirled, alert, axe handle at the ready, just in time to seize a small boy by the nape of his shirt and arrest his flight.

"Ha! I should'a thought of that closet. What were you doing in there?"

"Nothing."

"Nothing! Don't you remember what they said in town about always having an exit in case they came in? Hidin' in a closet. Look at your hands. And your mouth! What in the name of heaven is that truck?"

"I don't know, Aunt."

"Well, I know. It's jam—that's what it is. Jam that's supposed to stay down unmolested in the cellar in case the Zum come callin' in numbers. Forty times I've told you to leave those provisions alone. Hand me that switch."

The switch was a lot easier to wield than an axe handle and she was comfortable with the weight. The peril was desperate—

"Oh my! Look out behind you, Aunt!"

The old lady whirled around, sure she was about to find some green-skinned, horrible-smellin' Zum crawling up the front steps like a snail in the garden with no emotion on its face, and black, soulless eyes that no longer knew compassion. There was nothing. A curtain moved gently in the breeze.

The boy fled on the instant, out the front door, over the high board fence, and disappeared over it.

His aunt Polly stood surprised for a second, then broke into a gentle laugh.

"Hang the boy, can't I never learn a thing? Ain't he done me the same thing a dozen times and more? Can't learn an old dog new tricks, as they say. But for all that, how's a person to know what's comin' next? He knows he can torment me and get me all wound up inside, and he knows what with my constant worryin' about the undead maybe walkin' through the back door at any moment, all he's got to do is put me off or make me laugh, and I can't hit him a lick. I'm not doin' my duty by him, and that's the truth, goodness knows.

"He's full of the devil, but he's my dead sister's boy and I ain't got the heart to lash him, somehow. He was just a baby when one of the very first waves of Zum came through and kilt my sister dead. Scarcely found enough to bury, poor young thing. And with a baby left behind, unnoticed and untouched. Every time I put my mind on it, my old heart most breaks.

"But I'll make him work tomorrow to punish him. It's hard to make him work on a Saturday when all the other boys are having fun, but he hates work more than he hates anything else, and I've got to do my duty to him, or I'll be the ruination of that child."

Tom played hooky the rest of the day, and had a very good time. It was uneventful in such a way that would have relieved his aunt Polly greatly. He got home just in time to help Jim, a small colored child who lived with them, to saw the next day's wood and split kindling before supper—at least he was there in time to watch as Jim split the wood while Tom positioned himself on top of the woodpile to keep an eye out for trouble, of which there was none. Tom's younger brother (or rather, half brother) Sid, was already through with his chores for the day (boarding up the root cellar with long nails, leaving only enough room for some ventilation).

While Tom was eating supper, and stealing sugar as the opportunity afforded itself, Aunt Polly asked him questions that were full of guile and very deep—for she wanted to trap him as he had almost trapped himself earlier in the day in the dining room closet. Like almost everyone else on the planet, it was her cherished belief that she was endowed with a talent for mysterious diplomacy, and she believed her most obvious devices were marvels of impossible cunning.

"Tom, it was warm at school today, warn't it?"

"Yes'm."

"Powerful warm, warn't it?"

"Yes'm."

"But you still managed to learn a thing or two, right?"

"Yes'm."

"Well then," she said with delight, "tell us a thing or two you learned."

Sid let out a guffaw, enough to be noticed. He knew where Tom had spent the day, and it was not in school. He would not "out" his brother, but enjoyed the prospect of such a thing nevertheless.

Tom gave Sid a mean look.

"We learned different things all day long, Aunt Polly. Spelling. Adding, subtracting. Reading. Geography. Penmanship. History. About the Zum and what to do if you happen to bump up with them. I can't remember the whole day, Aunt Polly. You pick a topic and I'll tell you a thing I learned."

This was a bit of Tom's neat deflection. If Polly picked history, he could think of a fact or two. If she picked spelling, he could probably spell her a word. And he knew all he needed to know about the Zum, and was confident in that area. You stayed away from them, that was the gist of it. If you saw one in a field, you did not go into the field—and you found an adult with some experience in firearms. If one was skritching and clawing at your front door, you ran out the back. And you never, never let them get their hands on you. That was too horrible to even think about.

But Aunt Polly suddenly felt sorry for the boy. She felt

sorry for Sid. She felt sorry for herself. She even felt a brief pang for Jim, the small colored child she had taken to feeding in the kitchen. The fun was all gone, the game over for now.

"Oh bother! I'm sure you played hooky and went swimming, but I forgive you, Tom. It's no time in the history of things for begrudging a boy some small pleasure in life. You're like a singed cat—better'n you look as long as you don't take too deep a whiff. Get out, now."

But Sid saw his small pleasure evaporating before him, and he said: "Will you do nothing at all, Aunt Polly?"

Tom did not wait for the rest. As he went out the door, he said: "I'll lick you for that, Siddy."

Tom was not the model boy in the village. He knew the model boy very well, and had beaten him, one way or another, many times.

Within minutes, Tom had forgotten all his troubles. Not because his troubles were less heavy and bitter to him than a man's are to a man, but because a new and powerful interest drove these problems out of his mind. This new interest was a valued novelty that he had read about in the dime novels, and it consisted of calling out in the forest like a variety of birds. He could do the woodpecker, the mockingbird, the owl, and a variety of other woodland creatures. Or at least he thought he could. In truth, he did an excellent crow, but the majority of the other sounds bore a striking similarity. Tom and some other boys would creep up to a house, down in the weeds, and warble in a plaintive cry, and if the inhabitants didn't come rushing out and tell them to get the hell away from the house or they'd unloose some buckshot over their heads, they considered themselves successful. They would have dearly loved to come upon a lone Zum wandering through the woods and try their impersonations on it, but so far such a thing had not happened. As he strode down the quiet streets, Tom moaned and shrieked like a tropical bird or an egret. He felt much like an astronomer who has discovered a new planet, and as far as a cheap and reasonable pleasure was concerned, the advantage was with the boy making bird noises, not the astronomer.

Presently, Tom checked his birdcalls. A stranger stood before him—a boy slightly larger than himself. He didn't have the sliding, unnatural lurch of a Zum, so Tom felt no fear, just curiosity. A newcomer of any age or either sex was an impressive curiosity in their small village. When the Zum first made their appearance, a parade of doctors and wagons of soldiers came through the village, but as the phenomena was happening everywhere, it wasn't necessary to go out of your way to find them, and the parade ended.

The boy was well dressed. This was simply astounding. His cap was a dainty thing, and his entire ensemble was new and natty. He had shoes on—and it was only Friday. He even wore a bright bit of ribbon around his neck, which Tom found precious and off-putting. He had a citified air that ate into Tom's vitals like a host of hungry Zum. The more he stared at him, the shabbier his own outfit seemed to him to grow. Neither boy spoke. Both boys moved sideways—in a kind of circle, like wrestlers looking for an opening. Finally Tom said:

"I can lick you."

"Yeah, right. I'd like to see you try it."

"Well, I can do it."

"No, you can't either."

"Yes I can."

"No you can't."

"I can!"

"Can't."

"Can!"

"Look, we've pretty much exhausted the subject. You can't."

There was an uncomfortable pause. Tom changed tactics:

"What's your name?"

"Not any of your business, I think."

"Well, I 'low I'll make it my business."

"Well, why don't you?"

"If you say much more, I will."

"I believe we're covering much the same ground here."

Tom couldn't believe that his taunts were being so quickly dismantled.

"Say, what if I take a rock and bounce it off your head?"

"Sure you will."

"Well, I will."

"Well, why don't you then? Why do you keep *saying* you will for? Why don't you just do it? It's because you're afraid."

"I ain't."

"You are."

"Ain't."

"Are."

There are conservatively forty-seven distinct steps to combat in young boys, and Tom and the stranger were working through them as fast as they could. They were also being careful not to skip a step and move ahead with the combat, as that could spoil everything.

Tom said:

"You're a coward and a pup. I'll tell my big brother on you, and he'll thrash you with his little finger."

"What do I care about your big brother? I've got a brother, too—a bigger one—and what's more, he can throw your brother over that fence." (Both brothers were imaginary.)

"That's a lie."

"Isn't."

Tom drew a line in the dust with his big toe and said: "I dare you to step over that, I'll lick you till you can't stand up."

The new boy stepped over promptly and said:

"Now that you said you'd do it, let's see you do it."

"You'd better look out."

"Well, you said you'd do it—why don't you do it?"

"By jingo! For two cents, I *will* do it."

The new boy recoiled as if slapped with a recently used bath towel. "I don't have any money on me."

Tom smiled. It was a crucial turning point. "Hah!

That'll learn you. Better look out who you're foolin' with next time."

The new boy's face fell in confusion and defeat, and he backed off into the darkness, snuffling and muttering to himself, occasionally looking back and threatening what he would do the next time he found him out—and had two cents on him. As soon as Tom's back was turned, the new boy snatched up a stone, threw it, and hit Tom between the shoulders. Then he turned and ran home like an antelope. Tom chased him home, and thus found out where he lived. He held a position at the front gate for some time, daring his enemy to come back outside, but the enemy only made faces at him through the window and declined. At last the enemy's mother appeared and ordered him away, saying that his own poor mother must be worried sick that her stupid son was being disjointed and eaten somewhere by a ravenous Zum.

He got home late that night, climbed onto a shed next to the woodpile, and hoisted himself into one of the second-story windows. There he discovered his aunt, only half asleep, with an axe handle in her arms as if she were rocking a sweet newborn baby. When she woke and saw the state of his clothing, her resolution to turn his Saturday holiday into forced labor became adamantine in its firmness.

2

Tom Revises a Fence

Saturday morning came, and everything was bright and fresh, brimming with life. It was as though things had magically gone back to the way they were and there was nothing more to worry about than overdue library books, homework, and the relentless barking of stray dogs in the night. There was cheer in every face and spring in every step. The locust trees were in bloom and the scent of a million different blossoms filled the air. The landscape was green with new vegetation, ripe with promise, and the entire land was dreamy, content, and inviting. It was, of course, all a lie, but it was a sweet lie, one that could be overlooked and forgiven. The adults could stand watch from their porches and kitchen windows and savor it all like a sugary jawbreaker as long as they were aware it couldn't last. Guns and poles and machetes were close at hand. A cautious person could close his eyes for a few seconds and dream a bit.

Tom appeared on the sidewalk in front of his house with a wooden box filled with a variety of sharpened planes and whetstones. It was his aunt Polly's decision that he spend the day planing and sharpening the individual planks of their fence to make it a more formidable defense against the Zum rather than simply a cheery demarcation of property boundaries. It gave her a certain weary satisfaction to think that a number of invading Zum might somehow slip and impale themselves on the sharpened fence posts in an impetuous attack. Such a thing had never happened, but it seemed there was no reason why it couldn't. He surveyed the fence and all gladness left him and a deep melancholy settled down upon his spirit like a damp shroud. Thirty yards of board fence nine feet tall awaited him.

He admitted glumly to himself that Aunt Polly's decision made a kind of sense. You used a musket once, and then you were forced to withdraw to a more secure area to reload. The musket was not an accurate weapon, and when Tom went squirrel or possum hunting, the squirrel had as much to worry about from the loud report of the weapon as any subsequent damage. Boys would fire away at a tree'd possum for an entire afternoon and still come back empty-handed. As for the Zum, if you didn't hit the head with a clean shot, you only temporarily slowed their progress. It wasn't like they were going to bleed out and die, as they were already dead. Only a decent head shot put them down for good.

Sighing, Tom climbed on top of the wooden box and proceeded to put a nice tip on the end of a board with the wooden plane. The day was not yet hot, but it held the promise of some heat. Aunt Polly would bring him some lemonade when he had made sufficient progress. He repeated the operation and planed the tip of another board, then did it again. He compared the finished, sharpened tips of the few completed boards to the far-reaching continent of untouched fence and sat down on the wooden box discouraged. Soon, Jim came skipping down the road with a tin pail, singing "Buffalo Gals."

Bringing water from the town pump had always been hateful work in Tom's eyes before, as had coming along with a loaded gun to watch and guard. Now it did not strike him so. There were always other boys and girls at the pump, taking their turns, trading playthings, quarreling, skylarking, pretending to mow down line after line of the advancing undead with a single imaginary gun. And he remembered that, although the pump was only a hundred and fifty yards from his front door, Jim never completed his task in less than an hour—and even then, whoever was standing guard would usually grow bored and hurry him on. Tom said:

"Say, Jim, I'll fetch the water for you if you sharpen a board or two."

Jim shook his head vigorously and said:

"Can't, Marse Tom. Ole Polly tol' me I got to go an' git dis water an' not stop an' fool 'round wid anybody. She say she spec' Marse Tom gwin to ax me to poin' some boards, an' she tole me go 'long an' tend to my own bidness."

"I don't know, Jim. You heard there was some talk of some Zum spotted 'round the town pump, haven't you?" This was of course a lie, pulled from the great river of lies, but it was all Tom could come up with to make his own task seem at least comparatively more attractive.

"No, suh, Tom, I ain't heared such a thing. Anyway, them Zum is one thing. Your aunt with her feathers all ruffled up an' angry is another. I kin avoid one of 'em. Cain't avoid t'other."

"Oh, never mind all that, Jim. She always talks like that. Gimme the bucket—I won't be gone but a minute. She won't ever know."

"No suh, I dasn't, Marse Tom. Ole Polly would tear de head off'n me. Serious bidness indeed."

"Agwh! She never licks anybody—just whacks them over the head with her thimble—and who cares about a thing like that, I'd like to know. She talks a good game, but talk don't hurt. Anyways, it don't if she don't wind up cryin'. Jim, I'll give you a white marble I found."

Jim began to waver.

"Pure milk white, Jim. Looks like starin' into the eyes of a Zum, it does."

"My!" Jim exclaimed. He was almost sold.

"And I'll show you my sore toe."

Jim was only human, and this final attraction was too much for him. He loved staring at anthills, and beehives, and poking rotten logs and dead animals with sticks. It was the scientist in him. He put down the pail, snatched the white marble, and bent over the toe while Tom unwrapped the bandage. A moment later, Jim was flying down the street with his pail and a tingling sensation in his rear end, Tom was again planing the boards with vigor, and Aunt Polly was retreating from the scene with a wooden spatula in her hand and a look of utter triumph on her face.

But Tom's energy did not last—he began to think of the fun he would never have this day, and his sorrows multiplied. Soon, the other boys would be walking by to see what was going on, and they would make fun of him for having to work—the very thought of it burnt into his soul like the point of one of his sharpened planks. He took out his meager possessions and examined them—bits of this and that, a piece of string, other curious but worthless pieces of trash—and realized it would not be enough to buy the boys. He returned the treasures to his pocket and at this sad and hopeless juncture, an inspiration came to him.

He took up the plane and went contentedly back to work. Ben Rogers soon walked up—the very boy whose ridicule he had been dreading. Ben was lighthearted, his anticipation for the day high, and he was eating an apple picked from his own backyard. Periodically he would give out a long, melodious whoop, for just as Tom impersonated birds, Ben impersonated steamboats. Currently, he could only do two different steamboats, the *Horace E Bixby* and the *Captain H Mungus*, two almost identically sounding craft that occasionally docked nearby. He was encouraged in this enterprise, because when people were asked to guess which steamboat he was impersonating, they were generally correct. This was the happy result of having only two choices to pick from. The odds of a correct answer were very good.

"Stop her, sir! Ting-aling-aling!" Ben slowed and eased up to Tom and the fence. "Ship up to back! Up to back! Ting-aling-ling!" He came to a stop and stiffened down his sides. Tom knew the process of Ben's docking would be a long one, and so went back to his job. Eventually, when Ben's lines were secured and the engines had been shut down, Ben said:

"Hiya, Tom. You're up a stump, ain't you!"

No answer. Tom looked at the top of his most recently sharpened fence plank and surveyed it from several angles, eyeing it with the gaze of a satisfied artist. Ben came up next to him, but he stuck to his work. Ben said:

"Hey, they got you workin', eh?"

Tom looked startled and said:

"Why, it's you, Ben. I warn't noticing."

"I'm going swimming in a bit. Don't you wish you could? But of course you'd rather be standin' here sharpenin' stakes for the Zum to throw themse'fs on. You'd rather work—wouldn't you?"

Tom contemplated the thought for a moment and said:

"Depends on what you call work."

"Why, what you're doin' right now. I'd call that work."

Tom began concentrating on a new plank, gazing at the grain of the wood for inspiration, and answered carelessly: "Well, maybe it is, and maybe it ain't. All I know is, it suits me jus' fine."

"Oh, come on now. You mean to let on you like it?"

Tom's plane commenced to move, creating graceful curliques of wood shavings.

"Like it? I don't see why I shouldn't like it. Does a boy get a chance to work on a fort every day?"

That put the thing in a whole new light. Tom changed out the blade of the plane and pushed the sharpened tool across the board, increasing the angle on the point. He stepped back to note the effect—Ben standing, watching the procedure, getting more and more interested, more and more absorbed. Presently, he said:

"You don't think one of 'em'll just run themse'fs into one of these, do you?"

Tom started on another board and answered:

"Be a mistake if they did."

"Say, Tom, let me plane a board or two."

Tom considered it, rolled the idea around a bit in his head, but decided against it.

"Naw. I better not, Ben. It wouldn't hardly do. Aunt Polly's awful particular about what effect she hopes to accomplish with this fence. She must've had a dream about a porcupine, or some such. If it were the back fence, away from the street, I wouldn't mind, and I don't think she would either. But I don't think a boy in a thousand, maybe two thousand, would get it the way she has in her mind."

"That so. Well, just let me try. One board. I'd let you, if you was me, Tom."

"Ben, I'd like to, honest injun. But Aunt Polly, see—Jim wanted to try his hand, but she wouldn't let him. Sid wanted to do it, and she wouldn't budge. If I was to let you grab a plane and a board or two didn't get angled the right way—"

"Oh shucks. I seen you do it. I'll be just as careful. Gimme a plane. Lemme try. I'll give you my apple."

"Now Ben, don't. I'm afeered—"

"I'll give you a bunch of 'em!"

Tom gave Ben the plane with great reluctance, and while Ben began to sharpen board after board, Tom sat on an empty barrel in the shade, dangling his legs, munching on the first of many promised apples, every now and then surveying the landscape to make sure there was no imminent Zum attack. Although the undead were not in attendance, other boys happened by. By the time Ben was fagged out, Tom had traded the next chance to Billy Fisher for a kite, in good repair. And when he was played out, Johnny Miller bought in with the scrap of what was said to be a Zum shirt, covered with holes from many bullets and no little amount of blood. And so on and so on, hour after hour. By the end of the afternoon, Tom was literally rolling in a kind of wealth. Besides the treasures already mentioned, he had twelve marbles, a variety of startlingly white Zum teeth raked out of a pyre, a piece of broken blue glass that was said to have come from a burned-down church, a piece of chalk, a glass stopper from a liquor decanter, the last edition of a one-page newspaper from a small town nearby entirely burned and razed by the Zum, a tin soldier, a brass doorknob, the handle of a broken knife, several prayer cards of people killed in earlier attacks, and a handful of firecrackers.

The fence was now completely finished—the tips bristled menacingly—and had there been more sunlight in the day, Tom could have set up a second row of smaller stakes behind the first, at a slightly different angle.

Tom realized it was not such a bad world after all. Hordes of the undead roamed the world, intent on misery, horror, and destruction, but their efforts paled in comparison to what could be accomplished by the bored and the living. Their mindless, aimless rage was nothing to what could be accomplished by someone else's unstinting and earnest labor. Tom felt himself a great general, trampling all opposition in his path, and as the sun began to set and the streets cleared, he made his way back to Aunt Polly's headquarters to report his glorious victory.

3

Busy at Love and War

Tom presented himself before Aunt Polly, who was sitting by the narrow, confined openings of a window in a pleasant room farthest from the street. It was bedroom, breakfast room, dining room, and emergency exit to the root cellar all combined into one. The balmy, fragrant air and the drowsy murmur of the bees had had their effect, as had the convivial shouts and yips from the boys in the street, and she was nodding over her knitting, a cat asleep in her lap. Aunt Polly had great, intuitive faith in a cat's natural barometer for both calamity and tranquility, and when the cat was agitated, Polly was alert. When the cat decided there was nothing at all to worry about and it was a good time to sleep, Polly slept too. Her spectacles were propped up on her gray head for further safety. When she opened her eyes, she was somewhat puzzled at seeing Tom place himself in her power again. He said: "Mayn't I go and play, now, Aunt?"

She rubbed her eyes and looked at a wall clock. "What, a'ready? How much have you done?"

"It's all done, Aunt."

"Tom, don't you lie to me. I can't bear it."

"I ain't, Aunt. It's all done."

Aunt Polly placed small trust in Tom's sincerity. She shoo'd the cat off her lap, rousted herself out of the chair, and grabbed her axe handle to see for herself. She would have been pleased to find twenty percent of Tom's statement true. When she found the entire fence pointed and ready for an onslaught, the wood shavings raked up and piled in old peach baskets to use as kindling, her astonishment was almost unspeakable. She said:

"Well, I never. There's no denyin' you can do a thing when you set your mind to it, Tom." Her face beamed happily like a powerful porch light in an otherwise darkened neighborhood, and she diluted the compliment by adding: "But it's powerful seldom you set your mind to it, and that's the truth. Well, go 'long and play. Mind the sun. Mind anything that don't seem right. And get back home sometime in the next week, or I'll tan you."

She was so overcome by Tom's unexpected achievement that she grabbed an apple from a nearby crystal bowl and gave it to him, along with an impromptu lecture on virtuous effort, the kingdom of heaven, the goodness of honest sweat, and the wages of sin and corruption. On the way out the door, Tom "hooked" a doughnut.

Outside, he saw Sid unlocking the gate to the outside staircase that led to the back rooms on the second floor. Clods were handy, and the air was full of them in a twinkling. They fell about Sid like a hailstorm, and before Aunt Polly could collect her faculties and sally to the rescue, six or seven had found their intended mark, and Tom was gone. Usually, he would have hopped over the fence, but he was now unsure of the brutality of his morning's endeavor, and so he went through the gate. His soul was at peace.

Tom ran to the end of the block and was soon beyond the reach of his aunt's thrall, and went toward the public square of the village, where companies of boys had met for the day's combat. It was the favorite game of boys of Tom's age, and if it had a name, it would have been called "Us and Zum." Tom was currently one of the generals on one side, and Joe Harper (a bosom friend) one of the commanders of the Zum.

Each side had its advantages. Tom's side commanded platoons of cavalry and majestic, imaginary steeds, snorting and pawing the dirt, ready to ride into battle. The soldiers had wonderful imaginary uniforms, their lapels adorned with medals of past glory, and their imaginary sabers were incredibly sharp, their muskets accurate and never empty. There was a lot to be said about being on the other side, too. You could walk like a madman, snarling, spitting, rolling your eyes, and it was intoxicating if you came near a girl who might have been looking at you in school and she began to cry and begged you to stop. If you didn't (because you liked the attention), the soldiers on the other side could seize the initiative, and come up and pepper you with musket shot until you released the frightened girl. Later in the day, or perhaps the next time after she had calmed down, you could make amends by telling her you had shown mercy and spared her life, while you could have killed her on the spot and eaten her intestines.

At the end of the day's battle, Tom left the square and, as he passed the house where Jeff Thatcher lived, he saw a new girl in the garden—a lovely little blue-eyed creature with long, yellow hair plaited into two tails, a white summer frock, and embroidered pantalettes. The freshly crowned hero fell without a shot being fired. A certain Amy Lawrence fell out of his heart and vanished without a memory or trace left behind.

Tom had loved Amy to distraction, a passion and adoration that knew no bounds. He had taken months winning her heart, and her defenses had come down not a week earlier. He had been the happiest boy in the world for less than a week, and here in an instant she had gone out of his heart like a candle in a light wind.

He stared at this new creature until he saw that she had discovered him; then he pretended that he didn't know that she was present and began to "show off" in all sorts of ways to win her admiration. He kept up this grotesque foolishness for some time, until he glanced aside and saw the girl moving back toward the house. Tom's heart sank, and he began to grieve, hoping she would tarry awhile longer. She halted on the steps and moved toward the door. Tom heaved a great sigh, but his face lit up again, for she tossed a wildflower over the fence a moment before she disappeared.

The boy ran around the fence and stopped in front of the flower. Hesitating for only a moment, he snatched up the treasure and disappeared around the corner, where he buttoned the flower onto his lapel inside his jacket. He returned to his original post and hung about until nightfall, but the girl never showed herself again, though Tom comforted himself with the small hope that she had managed a peek out the windows and was thus aware of his presence. Finally, he ran home in the dark, his poor head full of visions and poetry.

All through dinner his spirits were so high that his aunt worried he might be coming down with some horrible new illness. He took a good scolding about pelting Sid with clods, and did not seem to mind it in the least. He tried to steal sugar out of the bowl under his aunt's very nose, and got his knuckles rapped for it.

"Aunt, you don't whack Sid when he takes it."

"Well, Sid don't torment a body the way you do. You'd be always int' that sugar if I warn't watching. And into worse, I'd imagine."

Presently, she stepped into the kitchen, and Sid, happy in his immunity, reached for the sugar bowl. But his fingers slipped and the bowl dropped and shattered on the wooden floor. Tom was in a kind of ecstasy. He told himself that he would not say a word, even when his aunt came in, but sit perfectly still till she asked who was responsible for the mischief. Then and only then he would tell, a bit haltingly, and there would be no feeling in the world so good as seeing his brother catch it. When the old woman came back and stood before the wreckage, crackles of discharged lightning and puffs of smoke seemed to dance over her spectacles.

He said to himself, "Here it comes!"

And the next instant, he was sprawled on the floor. Her hand was raised to strike again when he cried out:

"Hold on now, what'er you beltin' me for? It's Sid what did it."

Aunt Polly paused, but when she got her tongue back again, she only said:

"Umm. Well, then, it was good for somethin', I reckon. Like enough you're responsible for something around here to warrant it."

Then she fell silent and would have liked to say something kind and loving, but she realized it would have made her seem in the wrong, and so kept quiet. Tom retreated to sulk in a corner, fully aware that in her heart, Aunt Polly was mortified at what had happened, and he was dolefully gratified at this. He pictured himself lying sick unto death and his aunt bending miserably over him, beseeching him for a sign of forgiveness before he breathed his last and the Zum took over, invading his body to rise up again. How would she feel then? And he pictured himself brought home dead from the river, his curls all wet, his hair plastered to his head, his eyes rolled back. How she would have to be restrained from throwing herself on him in remorse and utter regret. How the tears would fall and her lips pray to

God to give her back her sweet boy and she would never do wrong to him again!

Of course there would be people to restrain her. For his eyes would open back up and he would grab anything within reach and try to tear it up into little pieces, to stuff it into his mouth, to consume it. He did not know why it was like this, but he knew it to be true. They would restrain her, and some adult would pop him in the head to put an end to all the foolishness, or take his head off with a handy shovel. This too, Aunt Polly would hold herself responsible for.

In considerable anguish, basking in misery, and eating it up with a long-handled ice-cream spoon, Tom went outside and wandered alone, down by the river. A small log raft called to him and he wished he could be drowned, all at once, without the horror and attendant unpleasantness of coming back as one of the dead. Then he remembered his cherished wildflower. He brought it out, rumpled and wilted, and he wondered if *she* would pity him when she spied him, roaming and grunting through the village with sunken eyes and torn, rotting flesh, until a sad delegation came out and ended his suffering and agony once and for all. It was such a rich scenario that he worked it over again and again in his mind, dying, rising up again, being struck down, again and again until he wore the whole thing thread-bare.

About ten o'clock, he came to the street where the Adored Unknown lived, and he paused a moment. No sound came to his listening ear. A candle flickered in a second-story bedroom. Was that her there? Was she thinking about him?

He lay down on the ground in front of the house with his hands clasped in front of him and holding the poor wilted flower. And thus he would have liked to die—out in the cold world, unloved, with no friendly hand to wipe away the final, trembling wetness from his brow, no loving face to bend mournfully over him to wait for his last moment and give the signal for the preemptive decapitation.

The window came up, and a maidservant pitched a deluge of water upon the poor boy's sacred remains.

Tom sprang up with a revived snort and galloped back home. As Tom climbed into the second-story window, surveying his drenched clothing by a single candle, Sid woke up, and wanted to say something chastising and adult, but thought better of it. Tom dried himself off and turned in without the added burden of prayer, and Sid made a mental note of the omission.

4

Showing Off in Sunday School

The sun rose upon a tranquil world and beamed down upon the cautious village like a blessing. There had been no calamities in the night. No alarm bells rang to roust the men from slumber into a nervous, armed pack. No distant shots echoed from afar, alerting everyone to *something* being out there. No gardens were trampled by horrible phantoms. No dogs barked at the moon and scratched at the doors to be let indoors, or being indoors, scratched to be let out.

Breakfast over, Aunt Polly had family worship; it began with a prayer built from the ground up with familiar scriptural quotations, and cemented with Polly's emotional sincerity. At the end of it, she threw in something about the final resurrection so her family wouldn't get the impression that this kind of thing was only bad and never something good.

Then Tom retired to a table in the sitting room and went to work trying to memorize his required verses. Sid had learned his days before. Tom bent all of his energies to the memorization of five verses that were from the Sermon on the Mount, because the only ones he could find that were shorter were too obvious in their brevity. "Jesus wept." He would save his supply of these for a day when he was a lot more desperate.

At the end of a half hour, Tom had a vague, general idea on what lesson the verses were trying to impart, but no more, for his mind was busy concentrating on any other thing it fell upon, and his hands were busy with other distracting recreations. His cousin Mary, who had recently come into town and was staying at the house, sat down next to him to hear his recital, and he tried his best to find a way through the fog:

"Blessed are the—a-a-"

"Poor . . ."

"Yes—poor—though I can't say I know for a fact why this is so—blessed are the poor—a-a-"

"In spirit . . ."

"In spirit, yes. Blessed are the poor in spirit, for they— they—"

"Theirs . . ."

"For theirs. Blessed are the poor in spirit, for theirs is the kingdom of heaven. Blessed are they that mourn, for they— they—"

"Sh . . ."

"For they—"

"Sh . . ."

"For they sh— Oh, I don't know what it is!"

"Shall!"

"Oh, shall! For they shall—shall mourn . . . a . . . blessed are they that shall mourn, for they shall—shall what? Why don't you tell me, Mary? What do you have to be so mean for?"

"Oh, Tom, you poor thick-headed thing. I'm not teasing you. I wouldn't do that. You'll manage it—really—and when you do, I'll give you something ever so nice. There now. Be a good boy."

"All right, then. What is it, Mary? Tell me what it is?"

"Never you mind, Tom. You know if I say it's nice, it is."

"You bet it is, Mary. I'll tackle it again."

And he did tackle it again, and this time, under the one-two punch of curiosity and prospective gain, he did it with such renewed concentration that he accomplished a re-sounding success. Mary was true to her word, and presented Tom with a brand-new "Barlow" knife worth twelve and a half cents. It came in a little wooden box that made it seem even more valuable. Pasted on top of the box was a picture of a grim-faced, buckskinned man, knife in hand, and an unholy throng of Zum staring at the knife, obviously fright-ened, retreating back into a black copse of trees.

Of course, the knife in the box wouldn't really cut any-thing, much less rout a host of Zum, but it was a Barlow sure enough, the blade made of high-carbon steel, and Tom ached to spend an afternoon with the knife on a good whet-stone to make it lethally sharp. Tom began to scarify the cupboard with it, and was beginning to eye the bureau when he was called away to dress for Sunday school.

Mary gave him a tin basin of water and a piece of soap, and Tom went outside the door and stared at the soap, loath to touch it. Presently he rolled up his sleeves, poured the water on the ground, and began to wipe his face with the clean towel. But Mary caught him in his activity and said:

"Now ain't you ashamed, Tom! You mustn't be so bad. Water won't hurt you." The basin was refilled and this time he stood over it, gathering resolution, and began washing. When he reentered the kitchen, there was an honorable testimony of suds and water dripping from his face. But when he emerged from the towel, he was still not satisfactory, for the clean territory stopped just short of his jaw. Below this line was a dark expanse of unirrigated soil that spread downward all the way to his toes. Mary took him in hand back outside, and when she was done with him, he was a man and a brother, and his saturated hair was neatly brushed. (Later, he privately plastered his hair close to his head to minimize his curls, for he held curls to be effeminate, and his own filled his life with bitterness.) Then Mary brought out a suit of his own clothing that had only been used on Sunday mornings for the last two years—they were simply known as his "other clothes." He now looked exceedingly improved and uncomfortable. He hoped Mary would forget about the shoes, but his hope was dashed. She coated them thoroughly with a mixture of tallow, as it was believed in some quarters that whatever it was that had infected the Zum wouldn't be able to crawl up your leg past a good thick coating of tallow. As Tom and most of the other boys only rarely wore shoes, this idea had been effectually debunked, but the custom went on. So he got into his shoes, and Tom was finally ready for Sunday school.

The school hours were from nine to ten thirty—and then the church service. Sentries who were also church elders posted themselves in front of the church and in the natural crow's nest of the church steeple, and Tom held that this was the perfect job for him, for it bordered on adventure and neatly sidestepped the whole issue of church attendance. At the door, Tom dropped back a step or two from the others and accosted a Sunday-dressed comrade:

"Say, Billy."

"Tom."

"You got a yaller ticket?"

"Yes, I do."

"What'll you take for it?"

"What'll you give?"

"Piece of lickrish and a fishhook."

"Well, let's see 'em."

Tom exhibited his wares, they were deemed satisfactory, and the property exchanged hands. Soon after, Tom traded more of the rich swag from the previous day's fence-pointing exercise—a couple of marbles for three red tickets, some small trifle for a blue one. He waylaid the boys as they came, and bartered for tickets of various colors ten or fifteen minutes longer. Then he entered the church with a swarm of clean and noisy boys and girls, and started a quarrel with the first boy who came handy. Tom pulled a boy's hair in the next bench and was absorbed by a hymnal when the boy turned around; he stuck a pin in another boy, in order to hear him say "Ouch!" and got an angry glare and silent reprimand from the teacher.

When it came time to recite their lessons, not one of the boys knew his verses perfectly, and each had to be helped along. However, each got his reward—in small blue tickets, each with a passage of scripture written on it. Each blue ticket was payment for two verses. Ten blue tickets equaled a red one, and ten red equaled a yellow one. For ten yellow tickets, the superintendent of the church gave a very plainly bound copy of the Bible to the pupil.

Who amongst us has the industry and application to learn by heart two thousand verses of the Bible? And yet Mary had acquired two Bibles this way—the patient work of two whole years—and a boy of German parentage had acquired four or five. It was a tragic story. The boy had a gift for memorization, and could recite the verses back for as long as people could stand to listen to them. However, his gift in this area seemed to come at a cost of plain common sense, and one quiet evening outside the village, fishing in a creek with no fish, he was set upon by several Zum, defending himself with only childish tears and uplifting verses from the Bible, neither of which had the desired effect. It was a grievous misfortune for the family, and a similar one for the school, for younger boys equated the memorization of Bible verses with bad luck and misfortune. Only the older students kept their tickets and stuck to the task long enough to get a Bible. It is likely that Tom never really hungered for such a prize, but rather the glory and rosy attention that came with it.

In due course, the superintendent stood up in the pulpit, cleared his throat loudly, and thus commanded the children's attention. The superintendent was a slim creature of thirty-five, with a sandy goatee and short, sandy hair. He had been to a religious college in England, years earlier, and was destined for a higher end in life, but as the shroud of the damn Zum settled itself on the world, he decided to forgo further chances of advancement that entailed travel and its dangerous companions. Mr. Killington was sincere and honest at heart, and he held the sacred and all things religious in such reverence that no one doubted his piety. After several rounds of throat-clearing that were strenuous enough that an adult might question his health, he began in this fashion:

"Now, children, I want you to sit up just as straight and pretty as you can and give me all your attention for a minute or two. I want to tell you how good it makes me feel to see so many bright, clean young faces assembled in a place like this, learning to do right and be good."

And so forth and so on. We have all had teachers like this, all destined for greater things and at some point resigning themselves to whatever they saw in front of them.

He was interrupted by the creak of the main church door and the entrance of visitors: Lawyer Thatcher, accompanied by a much older man, a portly gentleman with iron-gray hair. This was the lawyer's own brother, the great Judge Thatcher, recently returned from overseas. With him came a dignified, equally aged dowager who was doubtless his wife. The old lady came in leading a child—and when Tom saw the small newcomer, his soul burst into flames and all was bliss. The next moment he was showing off with all his might—cuffing boys, pulling hair, making grotesque faces—trying everything in his arsenal to fascinate a girl and win her applause.

The visitors were given the highest seat of honor, and as soon as Mr. Killington finished his little speech, he introduced the visitors to the rest of the school. The gray-haired old man turned out to be a prodigious personage—the kind of person Mr. Killington might have wished to be had he not shied away from constant travel. He was originally from a town some fifty miles away, but his spirit of adventure had taken him to the ends of the earth. He had been one of the first to travel to the Western shores of the continent, then to Hawaii, and thence to China, and it was a time in his life so rich in anecdote and adventure he only spoke of it with a cigar in one hand and a large whiskey in the other—in other words, only in front of adults. And while the life of an adventurer is already presumed to be full of peril, the arrival of the Zum was too much for his wife—especially now that they had a beautiful young daughter to think about—so he gathered up the two of them and left Asia once and for all and came back to the States. It was this spell-binding young creature who had captured Tom's heart and thrown him the cherished flower.

There was only one thing wanting to make Mr. Killington's whole year complete, and that was a chance to deliver a Bible prize and exhibit a prodigy to this special visitor. Several pupils had a few yellow tickets but none of them had enough. He would have given anything, anything to have that poor German boy back again. He knew this was a sin of pride, but couldn't help himself.

And now, when hope was all but dead, Tom Sawyer came forward out of the congregation, with nine yellow tickets, nine red tickets, and ten blue ones, and demanded a Bible.

Mr. Killington was familiar with Tom, not entirely in a good way, and was thunderstruck by the request. He had not expected a thing like this to happen with Tom for easily another ten years. But there was no getting around it—Tom had the colored chits and he was good for it. He was therefore elevated to a place with the missionary and his entourage, and the great news was announced from the pulpit. The other boys were eaten up by jealousy and envy—for they realized that they themselves had contributed to this miscarriage of justice by trading their tickets to Tom for the spoils he had accrued during the fence-pointing exercise. They despised themselves for being taken in by the dupes of a wily fraud, a guileful snake in the grass.

The prize was delivered to Tom with as much effusion as the superintendent could muster under the circumstances, but the poor fellow's instinct told him that there was a mystery here that could not bear the light. It was simply preposterous to believe that Tom had memorized two thousand verses—a dozen would have strained his capacity, without a doubt.

Amy Lawrence was proud and glad, and she tried to make Tom see it in her face—but he wouldn't look at her. He was too busy staring at the young girl sitting beside the two honored guests—and then it occurred to her what was happening and her heart broke. She was jealous and angry, and the tears came, and she hated everybody, Tom most of all.

Tom was introduced to the famous man, but his tongue was tied, his breath would barely come, and his heart quaked—not because of the greatness and range of the old man, but because of the young girl sitting next to him. He had never seen such beautiful eyes, such beautiful golden hair. He would have fallen down and worshipped her, but knew it would come to no good. The old missionary put his hand on Tom's head and called him a fine little man and asked him what his name was.

The boy had to turn his eyes away from the girl and concentrate on the face of the old man, and he managed to get it out:

"Tom."

"Ah. Very good. Very good indeed. But you've another name, I daresay, and you'll tell that one to me too, won't you?"

Tom had no idea what the old man was talking about, but Mr. Killington came to Tom's aid and interpreted:

"Tell the gentleman your whole name, Thomas. And say sir. You mustn't forget your manners."

"Thomas Sawyer—sir."

Tom stole another glance at the young girl and saw that

she was now looking at him. Her eyes were soft and kind, the color of a deep pool of clear water, and he believed he could stare at them for a day or two. The old man spoke again, as it seemed there was no stopping him.

"That's it! Good boy! Fine boy! Two thousand verses is a great many verses to learn—very, very many. And you will never be sorry for the trouble you took to learn them; it makes men good and good men great. You'll be a great man and a good one, someday, Thomas. You'll look back and say—yes, it's all due to my dear teachers who encouraged me to learn! That's what you will say, Thomas. And now would you mind telling me and my wife some of the things you've learned—now I know you wouldn't—for we are proud of our little boys who learn. Perhaps you have a favorite verse."

Tom knew the old man was speaking to him, and he nodded dutifully along as if he was paying attention, but it was too exhausting. He could only think of repeating his name and hope that pleased the old man.

"Are you familiar with Zechariah 14:12, son? The plague that turns the enemies of Jerusalem into Zum? Hah?"

Tom could only shrug his shoulders.

"Not one of your two thousand verses? Well, no problem. It goes something like this: 'Their flesh shall consume away while they stand on their feet, and the people will become like walking corpses. Their eyes shall shrivel in their sockets and their tongues shall decay in their mouths. And it will come to pass that on that day they will be terrified, stricken by the Lord, and they shall lay hold everyone on the hand of his neighbor, and his hand shall rise up against the hand of his neighbor.' "

This caught Tom's attention, and he was amazed he had never come across this passage before, and wondered if Aunt Polly was purposefully steering him away from the good stuff. He asked:

"What verse was that again?"

The old missionary was pleased to have found such a conscientious student, so keen on learning new things, and nodded approvingly to Mr. Killington, who had a much better handle on what was really going on. If there had been passages in the Bible about throwing firecrackers at cats or larking about with eggs in a bird's nest, Tom would have found these fascinating, too. Mr. Killington nodded in agreement and smiled back.

"Zechariah fourteen, verse twelve," he said.

"Zechariah fourteen, verse twelve," Tom repeated, wanting desperately to remember this. Had he known there were zombies and rotting flesh in the Bible, he might have tried a little harder to be a good student. Most of the verses he was familiar with were just admonishments to be good and kind and not do the things you felt like doing because they were most always wrong, and some kind of sin. His aunt had always steered him to the New Testament, and Tom realized he was himself partial to the Old.

"Well," the old missionary continued, "perhaps another verse would be in order. Would you tell us the names of the twelve disciples. Or perhaps the first two who were appointed?"

Tom was toying at a buttonhole and looked sheepish. He blushed now, and all eyes fell. Mr. Killington's heart sank within him. He thought it impossible that the boy could not answer the simplest of questions. He felt obliged to speak.

"Answer the gentleman, Thomas. Don't be afraid."

And before he could stop himself, Tom blurted out:

"David and Goliath!"

It was to all intents and purposes the end of that morning's instruction.

5

The Pinch Bug and His Prey

About half past ten the sentries came down the church steeple briefly to ring the church bell, and people began to gather for the morning's sermon. The Sunday school children distributed themselves about the house and occupied pews with their parents, so as to be under their supervision. Aunt Polly arrived, and propped her ubiquitous axe handle in the corner of the vestibule, testimony to her belief that nothing could happen to her in this sacred place. Tom and Sid and Mary sat with her—Tom on the aisle, in order to make him as far as possible from the open window and its seductive attractions.

The crowd filled the church, some common figures seen here and there around the village, others less common and seen almost exclusively at worship: the aged postmaster who had seen better days, but curiously had never, ever seen a

Zum; the mayor and his wife, who lived happily on a large estate far outside the village proper and kenneled a number of large, serious dogs for hunting and home defense; the justice of the peace, who as an instrument of law and order found himself responsible for maintaining a list of men who could be called upon to gather, without fail, even in the middle of a wet night, in defense of the town; the Widow Douglas, fair, smart, and forty, her hill mansion the ultimate place of refuge for all should such a thing be required. After the tragic death of her husband—so foul that it was only alluded to—she directed her energy to creating an impenetrable fortress, complete with guard towers, catwalks, munitions, multiple larders, and underground bunker. It had never been used in this capacity, but the townspeople found it a relief to know that such a thing existed should circumstances dictate.

Next came the belle of the village, cool and pleasantly moist, fanning herself with a paper fan, followed closely by a troop of ribbon-decked young heartbreakers, and then all the young male clerks in town in a body. They stood in the vestibule till the last girl had entered and run their gauntlet. Last of all came the model boy, Willie Mufferson, bringing in his mother as if she were made out of cut glass. He always brought his mother to church and was the pride of all the matrons. The men were not as impressed. Because of his dotage on his mother, he could never be counted on to go out with the men when the Zum might be about. His white handkerchief was hanging rakishly out of his pocket, and Tom, who had no white handkerchief, resented him and looked on him as a snob. The men also found him qui-etly unsavory, for much different reasons.

The congregation was fully assembled now and the church bell rang a final time, to warn stragglers outside that they were now more or less on their own, and to alert the sentries outside that church was now in session, and their vigilance was now more necessary than before.

The minister gave out the hymn and read it through with a relish, in a peculiar style that was all his own. His voice began on a medium key and climbed steadily up till it reached a certain point, then plunged down as if from a springboard:

> *Shall I be car-ri-ed to the skies, on flow'ry beds*
> *Of ease*
> *Whilst others fight to win the prize, and sail thence to bloody*
> *Seas?*

Tom understood that the minister was a wonderful reader, for others said so, but he almost never followed what he was talking about, especially when it came to the sermon. Listening to the old hymn, Tom appreciated the melody, but had no interest in the message. His ears perked up when he heard the words "fight" and "bloody seas," but almost immediately realized it was a bit of poetic license, and there would be no discussions of such things. The ladies in the congregation also enjoyed this, for it *was* poetic license, and their lives held too little poetry. It was a flowery respite.

After the hymn had been sung, the Rev. Mr. Sprague

turned himself to a bulletin board and read off "notices" of meetings and societies and things that were either note-worthy or queer until it seemed the list would go on until the crack of doom. The shank of the queer information was Zum-related. A farmhouse in the next county had burned to the ground—blankets and donations were joy-fully accepted—and the Zum were held suspect. A Zum had been pulled out of the river, quite accidentally, as he had been caught under a log for several days, and while in the process of being pulled out, was still active and had to be dispatched. A pack of feral dogs had torn the legs off a Zum and several had gotten sick on the meat, but had re-covered and had not changed over to that accursed state. The largest of the cities across the state were coping better than they had at the beginning of the outbreak—there was legislature now on the books concerning the prompt dis-posal of dead bodies, and the universities were studying the whole phenomena, looking for answers.

And now the minister prayed. A good generous prayer it was, and went into details: it pleaded for the church itself and the poor, innocent children of the village; for the men who were guarding the church; for other churches in the village and for the village itself; for the churches across the United States; for Congress, for the president and the many fine men and women in the military; for the heathen in for-eign lands who, as far as anyone knew, were also suffering and dying under the Zum curse; and for the Zum them-selves who had once been God's creatures, citizens and neighbors, before coming to this foul end. And he ended that the words he was about to speak might be as seed sown on fertile ground, yielding in time a harvest of good. Amen.

There was a rustling of dresses, and the congregation sat down. Tom did not enjoy the prayer, but rather endured it. He stood restive through it, not really listening, and when any new matter was interlarded, his ear detected it for a few moments until his concentration strolled elsewhere. In the midst of the prayer, a fly lit on the back of the pew in front of him. It calmly rubbed its hands together, embracing its head with its arms and polishing it so vigorously that it seemed to almost part company with it. Tom stared at the fly and wondered why the God they were all praying to had created such a thing. They were ugly beasts, useless really, seeming to spend their days resting in cow flop or sitting on the dining room ceiling while you ate your Sunday dinner. They disappeared in winter and returned again in the spring. They did not sow, neither did they reap. Tom reasoned he would have made a god at least as good as this. No more houseflies. No more ticks. No more mosquitos. No more Zum. No more Sunday school. No more warts. No more toothaches, no more sorrow . . . It was blasphemous, he knew, but try as he might he could find nothing wrong with the idea. The moment the minister said "Amen," Tom snatched the fly from the back of the pew with an open hand as he sat down, but his aunt detected the subterfuge, and poked him in the ribs to let it go.

The minister began reading the sermon and it was so even-keeled and prosy that many a head by and by began to nod. It was an argument that dealt with fire and brimstone and eternal damnation, thinning the preordained select down to a company so small as to be hardly worth the effort. Tom counted the pages of the sermon, and after church always knew how many pages in the sermon there had been, but he seldom remembered anything else about the discourse. However, this week he was really interested for a little while. The minister made a grand and moving picture of all the world's people, living and dead together, coming together at the millennium, all standing in front of the throne of God on that last day to be judged.

Tom wondered if the Zum would be damned outright for their activity, or would their punishment be lessened depending on the people they had been before their transformation. Did one activity cancel out the other? No one *wanted* to be a Zum. If you became one that killed and savored human flesh, would that be more punishable than if you were a Zum who was just shot walking through someone's cornfield? Were the Zum accountable at all? And to who? Or was it whom? The horror of this grammatical dilemma made him retreat back to his current circumstance.

The sermon continued, and presently he remembered a treasure he had and got it out. It was a large black beetle with formidable jaws—a "pinch bug." He had found it that morning and put it in the little wooden knife box that Mary had given him. The first thing the beetle did was bite him on the finger. Tom jerked his hand back and the beetle flew into the aisle and lit on its back, the hurt finger went into the boy's mouth. The beetle lay there, working its helpless legs, unable to turn over. Tom eyed it and longed for it, but it was well out of his reach. Other people in the congregation found relief in the beetle, and they eyed it too. Presently, a dog from the village came idly down the aisle, lazy with the summer and the heat, and spied the beetle. He surveyed the prize; walked around it and smelt it from a close distance.

Growing bolder, he took a closer smell, then lifted his lip and took a gingerly nip at it, just missing it. He tried again. Eventually, he went to his stomach with the bug between his paws, batting it playfully whenever it tried to make a dash. Growing weary at last, his head descended and touched the beetle, who immediately seized it. There was a sharp yelp, and the beetle flew a few yards away, on its back once more. There was resentment in the dog's heart now, and a craving for revenge. He jumped at it from different angles, making even closer snatches at it with his teeth. But he grew tired once more and tried to amuse himself with a fly. Wearying of that, he yawned, sighed, forgot the beetle entirely, and sat down on it to listen to the rest of the sermon. Then there was a wild howl of agony and the dog went flying up the aisle, down a side aisle, until he was but a scrawny, woolen comet looking for an open door. He sprang upon his owner's lap, and this person flung it out an open window. The voice of distress quickly thinned out and died in the distance.

By this time the whole church was red-faced and snorting with suppressed laughter, and the sermon came to a dead standstill. When it was resumed, it went lame and halting, lurching to its conclusion like one of the undead brought back to life. It was a relief to everyone when the ordeal was over and the benediction pronounced.

Tom Sawyer came home quite cheerful, for it was now Sunday afternoon, and it would be another week before the whole unnatural thing repeated itself. He put on his regular clothes, put his Sunday clothes on the bed, where Mary might do the right thing and put them neatly away, and kicked his shoes underneath the mattress. Not wanting to take responsibility for the pinch bug, the howling dog, or anything else that happened in church that morning—including an explanation to Aunt Polly on how he had obtained his new Bible—he clambered out a window, hopped down to the woodshed, and ran out of the yard before anyone knew he was gone.

6

Tom Meets the New Girl

Monday morning found Tom miserable. Monday morning always found him so—because it began another week's suffering in school. He generally began that day wishing there had been no intervening holiday, as it made the descent into captivity and fetters so much more odious.

Lying in bed, it occurred to him that an illness would keep him home from school. It was at least an idea, the *germ* of an idea, and he canvassed his system. No ailment was found, and he investigated again. There was nothing he could point to that seemed to indicate a defect in the system. Suddenly he discovered something. One of his upper teeth was loose. He could push it forward with his tongue and suck it back again. He did this several times. He was about to groan and put all of his money on this symptom, when it occurred to him that if he pushed all of his chips into the pot with this tooth, his aunt would pull it out, and that would hurt. So he sucked the tooth back into its original position and pushed it down slightly with his tongue to re-cement it. Nothing else came to him for some time, and then he remembered hearing the village doctor tell about losing one of his patients to the Zum after two or three weeks of the patient losing his fingers and toes to gangrene. So the boy drew one foot out of his sheet and held it up for inspection. The big toe was pink and a little swollen, but not hard or painful at all. Luckily, Tom was not aware of the various symptoms of gangrene other than the final one, and assumed pink and slightly swollen would be enough to at least spend one day away from school.

He began moaning, first just like it was some bad dream where undead monsters came ranging across the landscape after him, but there was no result from his brother, who lay asleep in bed, so he moaned with a bit more gusto. He opened his mouth and groaned aloud, loud enough to be talking across a room, but Sid snored on.

Tom was aggravated. He hopped out of bed and said "Sid, Sid!" shaking him by the shoulders. This worked much better. Sid yawned, brought himself up on an elbow, and began to stare at Tom, who fell back on his bed and continued to groan.

"Tom! Tom! What's the matter?"

Tom moaned and thrashed around on his bed.

"Tom!" Sid asked again, shaking his brother and peering into his face with some concern.

Tom's eyes fluttered open and he moaned again as preface.

"Oh, don't, Sid. Don't joggle me so."

"Why? What is it, Tom? I must call Auntie."

"Oh, don't, Sid. Don't call nobody."

"But I must! It's awful! How long you been this way?"

"Hours. Ouch! My whole body is in pain, Sid. Don't stir so. It's killing me."

"Oh, Tom, why didn't you wake me sooner? It makes my flesh crawl to hear you, Tom. You suppose you're dyin?"

Sid was no doctor and Tom the perfect, compliant patient for him.

"I forgive you everything, Sid. Everything you've ever done to me. And when I'm gone—"

"No, Tom! Don't die on me now!"

"When I'm gone, tell 'em. Tell 'em I forgive everybody. You'll get the knife Mary brought me—it's not really sharpened yet. You'll have to do that. And the new girl in town, tell her—"

But Sid had heard enough. He snatched up his clothes and was gone. He flew downstairs and said:

"Oh, Aunt Polly, Tom's dyin'!"

"Dyin'?" It had been such a nice peaceful morning so far. She was having a cup of chicory, staring off out the window, utterly at peace.

"Yes'm. Please, come quick!"

"Rubbish!" she replied, her pleasant morning dashed to pieces, but she got up from her chair, put down the chicory, gathered up her axe handle, and told Mary to run and fetch the doctor.

Aunt Polly's face grew white, and her lips trembled as

she climbed the stairs. It was too much for her. Losing the mother first and now perhaps the son. It wasn't right, and it wasn't fair. She longed for a scriptural verse to give her a moment's comfort, but nothing came to her. There were too many images pushing into her mind of what was going to happen next—the foul breath; the reddened, rheumy eyes; the twitching of the eyelids; the awful clenching of the body; then a brief relaxation as the spirit escaped and left behind an empty husk for the Zum to inhabit. There was only a short window of time available to grieve and say good-bye. If the loved ones took too long and lingered over the body, it would soon begin to twitch again, the horrible reincarnation would commence its course, and she would have to treat the boy as one of them. Sometimes it took minutes, sometimes as long as a day. If the doctor made it back to the house in time, he could take a sharp scalpel to the head, slice it through and disconnect it. It was an unsavory thing, but it would stop the inevitable. Then there could be enough time for a proper funeral, a wake, and a Christian burial. Things could still be salvaged. Tom would have to wear a tie.

When she reached his bedside, she saw that he was still among the living, and gasped out:

"Tom! Oh, Tom, my boy, what's the matter with you?"

"Oh, Auntie, I'm—"

"What's the matter with you, child?"

"Oh, Auntie, it's my big toe. It's mortified!"

Aunt Polly threw off the covers, expecting a fresh horror,

but found a healthy, pink toe. She sank down into a chair and laughed a little, then cried a little, then did both together. She looked at Sid, who was standing unsteadily in the doorway.

"Sid, run along after Mary and tell her it's all right. We won't be needin' the doc." Sid disappeared without a word, just glad to be doing something necessary.

The boy felt a little foolish, and he said:

"Aunt Polly, it *seemed* mortified. I thought I *was* dyin'. How's a person to know?"

Indeed, how could anyone know? Aunt Polly knew she could not explain it. The gulf between the living and the dead was unknowable; that was why there was religion, and an attendant faith in things that could in no way be proven. It provided a convenient mortar to make the rest of the world stay together. The gulf between death and the horror of the subsequent, inevitable Zum infestation was beyond unknowable—it cracked the mortar religion had provided, and the world fell again into pieces. Knowing that everyone in the world would someday come back as a rotting horror beyond imagination put a seed of hopelessness in a person's world that could not be excised. No one could explain the phenomena. You could live with it, and deal with it, but you could not stare at the thing too long.

Aunt Polly had already forgiven the boy, and was happy he was still alive. In celebration, she went back downstairs and made them all hot biscuits for breakfast, and that is how Tom lost his wobbly tooth—by biting greedily into a fresh biscuit. But losing a tooth is nothing like losing a son, and Polly gave him a second biscuit and pushed him out the door toward school.

As Tom wended his way to school, he was the envy of every boy he met because the gap in his upper teeth enabled him to expectorate in a new and charming way. He gathered quite a following with his exhibitions. Another boy, who had also "almost died" that morning with a cut on his finger, found himself with a lesser following. Dying of a finger wound was just no match for an infected toe, losing a tooth, and being able to spit like a cobra. His heart was heavy and he said it was nothing at all to spit like Tom Sawyer, but another boy said "Sour grapes!" and he wandered away a healthy, if distracted hero.

Shortly, Tom came on the juvenile pariah of the village, Huckleberry Finn, son of the town drunkard. Huckleberry was cordially hated and dreaded by all the mothers of the town, for he was idle and lawless and vulgar and bad. All the children of the village admired him for these exact same qualities, and wanted to be like him. Huck's father also bore another curious distinction—besides being a notorious drunk, he was also the only man in the village—and perhaps anywhere else—to get into a fistfight with one of the Zum. He had not realized the thing approaching him was one of the undead, and had taken the approach as a challenge, and drunkenly started throwing punches. Most of his other senses had failed him, but not his jab or his haymaker. He could not hurt his opponent, but did an excellent job of fending it off. Much later, when recounting his adventure over a mug of cider, he admitted that he quite admired his adversary's ability to take a punch, but after fifteen minutes of unbridled mayhem, reinforcements arrived and dispatched his sparring partner by lopping its head off with a sharpened saber. Immediately thereafter, Huck's father passed out and slept for fifteen hours. The doctor conferred with other medical specialists and wondered aloud if something in a drunkard's system—perhaps the amount of alcohol present—made him somehow immune to the Zum. The idea was soon dismissed, as testing it would have entailed a series of experiments that no one wanted to be held responsible for putting together.

Home life for Huckleberry was, as one might suspect, not the best. He came and went at his own free will. He slept in doorways in fine weather and empty hogsheads in wet. He did not have to go to church or to school, or call any being master or obey anyone else. He could go fishing or swimming whenever he chose, and stay at whatever interested him for as long as he liked. Perhaps because of this, he had crossed paths with the Zum a number of times, and as a result did not highly estimate their talents or abilities. The mothers of the village opined that he lived among them with a peculiar freedom, as their habits and scents were probably much the same. He was always the first to go barefoot in the spring, and the last to resume leather in the fall. He never had on clean clothes. He could swear wonderfully. In a word, he was an exemplary boy, to another boy.

Tom hailed the romantic outcast.

"Hello, Huckleberry."

"Hello yourself."

"What's that you got there?"

"Dead cat."

"All dead or mostly dead?"

Huck picked up the sad, unfortunate pile of fur and gave it a gentle shake, as if to awaken it. "So far all dead, but you never know. It might come back."

Tom took a closer look at the cat. "I didn't think animals did this. Never seen no Zum cow or anything. I figgered they just stayed dead."

Huck shrugged his shoulders. "Either way, I'm ready." He held up a rough leash fashioned out of a heavy twine. He had never owned a pet, and marveled that people actually remembered to feed and water them at conscientious intervals. A Zum cat would need no such special treatment, and would have thus been perfect.

"Whose was it?"

"No one's. It was free."

"Where'd you get him?"

"Bought him off a boy."

"Fer what?"

"Some blue church tickets and a bladder I got at the slaughterhouse. I told him the bladder came from a Zum. Could'a sold a dozen such."

"Say, what's a dead cat good for, Huck?"

"Good for? Good luck, mostly. Keeps the Zum away. They cain't hardly stand to be around them."

"Why's that?"

"Now how would I know the answer to that? I just know it t'be true."

"Better than spunk water?"

"Spunk water? I wouldn't give a dern for spunk water."

"You wouldn't, would you? D'you ever try it?"

Huckleberry made a pained face. "No, I hasn't. And I don't think I ever will. Spunk water's for riddin' yourse'f of warts and such, not for drivin' away them spooky Zum. But you get yourself a dead cat, you might as well be invisible to 'em. They'll walk all around you and not disturb you in the least. You just take your cat and git to a graveyard around midnight when there's a full moon so you can see what's about. When it gets to be midnight, you'll *hear* the Zum but not see 'em, like somethin' bad on the wind. When the sound dies down and it gets quiet, that's when you spin your cat around, holdin' ont' its tail. Spin it three times and say 'Zum-bies, Zum-bies, Zum-bies, foller this cat to hell! I'm done with ye! Leave us alone and go somewheres else.' That'll do the trick."

"Sure sounds right. D'you ever try it, Huck?"

"No, but old Mother Hopkins told me about it. And she's a witch, a true one. You won't ever see the Zum messin' about with her. She witched my pap, too. He seen her on the road, a-witchin' him, so he took up a rock, and if she hadn't dodged, he'd 'a' gotten her. Well, that very night he rolled off'n a shed where he was layin' drunk, and broke his arm."

"That's awful. How did he know she was a-witchin' him?"

"Lord, Pap can tell, easy. Pap says when they keep lookin' at you, they're a-witchin' you. 'Specially if they mumble. Because when they mumble, they're sayin' the Lord's Prayer backwards. Gimme a handful of Zum any day over some evil witch. I see Mother Hopkins in the road I take off my hat and say 'good evenin'' and keep on goin'. I see me some Zum, I find some good-sized rocks to peg at 'em."

"Say, Huck, when you goin' to try the cat?"

"Tonight. It's a full moon, so I may as well. 'T'will be a good test."

"Lemme go with you?"

"Of course, if you ain't afeared."

"Afeared? 'Tain't likely. You got your bird calls down?"

"I do."

"Good. We'll chirp at each other so we know where we both are."

"All right then." Tom left Huck practicing his cat spin incantations and strode off to school.

When Tom reached the little isolated schoolhouse, he went past old Mr. Branson, the retired gentleman who watched out at the school every day as a courtesy with his aged but effective blunderbuss. Mr. Branson was taking a little nap in the morning sun, but opened his eyes briefly when he heard Tom's approach, and waved him inside. Tom hung his hat on a peg and flung himself into his seat with businesslike alacrity. The schoolmaster was roused by the sound of the closing door.

"Thomas Sawyer!"

Tom knew that when his name was pronounced in full, it meant trouble was looking for him or had just found him.

"Sir!"

"Come up here. Now, sir, why were you late again this morning?"

Tom was about to take refuge in a lie, when he saw two long tails of bright blond hair hanging down a back and was immediately smitten by the electric sympathy of love; and next to her was the only vacant seat on the girls' side of the schoolhouse. He instantly said:

"I stopped to talk to Huckleberry Finn!"

The master's pulse stood still and he stared helplessly. The buzz of quiet study ceased. The pupils wondered if this foolhardy boy had lost his mind. The master said:

"You—you did what?"

"Stopped to speak to Huckleberry Finn."

There was no mistaking the words.

"Thomas Sawyer, this is the most astonishing confession I have ever listened to. Take off your jacket."

The master grabbed a switch and performed until his arm was sore. Then the order followed.

"Now sir, go and sit with the girls! Let this be a warning to you!"

The titter that rippled through the classroom appeared to abash the boy, but in reality, that result was caused more by the success of his operation and the close proximity to his unknown idol. He sat down at the end of the bench and the girl hitched herself away from him with a toss of her head. Soon the attentions ceased, and he began to steal furtive glances at the girl. She observed it, and gave him the back of her head for a minute. When she turned around again, a peach lay before her. She pushed it away. Tom patiently returned it to its place. She pushed it away, but with less animosity. Then he began to draw something on his slate, hiding the work with his left hand. Her curiosity overcame her, and she made an attempt to see it, but the boy still shielded his work. Presently she whispered:

"Let me see it."

Tom partially uncovered a dismal caricature of several houses, one with flames pouring through the windows. There were several monster stick figures marching toward the house, their hands straight out before them like sleepwalkers. Tom drew himself in front of the house, defending it with musket and sword, but of course it looked like another monster stick figure facing a different direction.

She seemed pleased with the drawing and said:

"It's ever so nice. Shall I draw you a picture?"

He said not a word, but handed her the slate. He wiped his picture off so as not to put her in an awkward situation. She drew a ship sailing on the water, more monstrous stick figures, and Tom took from it a sense of isolation and loneliness.

"It's good. Do you have to go to dinner?"

"I don't have to. I'll stay if you'll stay."

"Good. We'll draw us some more. What's your name?"

"Becky. Becky Thatcher. My father is the judge."

"Oh really?" Tom responded, as if he had not already known that.

She nodded her head. "I know your name. It's Thomas Sawyer."

"I'm Tom, Becky. Thomas is what they use when I'm about to be licked."

She smiled at the boy like he had uttered some great joke.

Now Tom began to scrawl something else on the slate, hiding the words from the girl. She was not shy this time, and leaned over him to see what he was writing. Tom said:

"It ain't nothin'."

"Yes it is. Let me look."

"You'll tell."

"No I won't—ever."

"As long as you live?"

"I won't tell anyone. I promise."

And she put her small hands on his and a little scuffle ensued, Tom pretending to resist, but letting the slate fall until the words were revealed: I LOVE YOU.

"Oh, you liar!" she said, not minding it at all, her face reddened and pleased. Tom and Becky made an attempt to study the rest of the afternoon, but the turmoil in both of them was too great. They drew each other pictures on the small slates, and the pictures were collections of things too important and dramatic to put into words. Neither of them were artists, but each had the feeling the other understood what things they were trying to convey. Several times the master asked Tom a question, and Tom answered poorly, turning lakes into rivers, rivers into mountains, and mountains into continents. When the master moved on, Tom drew a picture on the slate—a picture of the master—and Becky leaned closer and smiled fondly.

7

Insect Wars and Heartbreak

The harder Tom tried to fasten his mind to his book, the more his ideas wandered. So at last, with a sigh and a yawn, he gave it up. The air was utterly dead, without a hint of sweetness or breeze. It was the sleepiest of sleepy days. Away in the blinding sunshine, the little village lifted its soft green side through a shining veil of heat; a few birds floated high in the air; no other living thing was visible but some cows off on the side of a hill, and they were motionless, asleep. His hand wandered into his pocket, and his face lit up in surprise. He had forgotten that he'd captured yet another pinch bug that morning and imprisoned it in the empty wooden knife box. The released pinch bug lay on the long flat desk—and right side up, which was fortuitous. The creature probably glowed with a gratitude that approached bug prayer, but it was premature: for when it began to travel off, Tom turned it aside with a pin—minding that his fingers were safely out of the way—and made him march in a new direction.

Tom's bosom friend crept over and slid next to him, suffering with boredom as Tom had been suffering, and he was instantly, gratefully interested in this new entertainment. This bosom friend was Joe Harper. The boys were sworn friends all week and passionate enemies on Saturdays. Joe took a pin out of his lapel and began to assist in exercising the prisoner. Soon Tom said they were interfering with each other, and told Joe to look around the floor of the schoolroom and find another insect. Then each would have his own combatant in this arena. Tom took the slate and drew a line down the middle of it from top to bottom. He thought he was being wonderfully democratic.

"Now," he said, "you start one on your side, I'll start mine on my side, and we'll see whose is strongest, or fastest."

Joe looked around the room in exasperation and could find nothing.

"That's not fair, Tom. The room's been cleaned. 'Tain't no bugs. Let's just play with yours."

Tom pulled the slate closer to his chest. "No. This one is mine, Joe. You find another." Joe was angry in a minute.

"There ain't no more pinch bugs in here, Tom. You got the only one. C'mon!"

"Well then, find somethin' better."

Joe surveyed the room and the walls of the building. The master was almost dozing in his seat, woozy with the oppressiveness of the day, so getting up and moving around was an option. But there were no decent competitors to be found. There were a few flies buzzing around the window, but flies were wild and untrainable. Even crippled and in danger of being swatted to extinction, they would not heel. There was a lone wasp in one high corner of the room, but wasps would not play at all. The spiderwebs were old and abandoned and there was nothing there. Finally, Joe picked up a working black ant from the floor and brought him to the arena. The two insects ignored each other. Tom kept turning the pinch bug back toward the middle of the slate, as did Joe. They both knew there was a terrific match here if the insects would just recognize it. At one point, the ant began to crawl *over* the pinch bug, and though it was not the result they were going for, it seemed like a decent bit of progress.

It was during this period of absorption that a tremendous whack came down on Tom's shoulders and another one on Joe's. The master was awake now, and laid into the boys for several minutes. The whole class enjoyed it and was wonderfully revitalized. The master had come tiptoeing down the room while Tom and Joe were herding their insects and goading them into battle, and watched a good part of their performance before he contributed to it.

When school broke up at noon and everyone was freed, Tom flew to Becky Thatcher and whispered in her ear.

"Put on your bonnet and say you're goin' home. When you get to the corner, turn down through the lane and come back here. I'll do the same."

She agreed, and one went off with one group, the other

with another. In a while, the two met at the bottom of the lane, and when they reached the school, they had it all to themselves. Then they sat together, again with a slate between them, and Tom gave Becky a pencil and held her hand to guide it, creating another unusual drawing. When the interest in art began to wane, the two fell to talking. Tom was swimming in bliss. He said:

"Do you love rats?"

"No! I hate them."

"Well, I do too. Live ones, I mean. But how about dead ones, to swing over your head with a string?"

"No, I don't care for rats at all, alive or dead. The judge says I am not to touch rats, as it's his opinion that the Zum plague is carried that way."

"Well, how 'bout spiders?"

"No. I don't care for spiders, either. The webs are nice, when you see them outside in the morning, after a rain."

"Ever see a spider as big as this?" He drew a large, smiling spider on the slate that was very disturbing.

Becky shook her head. "No. But I've seen a tiger."

Tom was incredulous. "At a circus?"

"No. Overseas." She waved with her hand as if it was a place just on the other side of the door, somewhere outside.

" 'Cause I've been to the circus. Lots of times. There's things goin' on at a circus all the time. Fat ladies and jugglers and clowns. I'm goin' to be a clown in a circus when I grow up."

Becky just nodded her head to show she was paying

attention, but she was disappointed that Tom had shown so little interest in pursuing the tiger story and her origins. She had come from overseas. She had seen a tiger. The boy who had played with an insect all morning hadn't found this interesting.

"They make plenty of money—'most a dollar a day, Ben Rogers says. You met Ben yet?"

Becky shook her head again.

"You will. Say, Becky, was you ever engaged?"

"What's that?"

"Why, you know, engaged to be married?"

"No."

"Would you like to?"

"I don't know. What is it like?"

"Like? Why, it ain't like anything. You just tell a boy you won't ever have anyone else but him, ever ever *ever*, and then you kiss, and that's it. Anyone can do it."

"Kiss? What's the kiss for?"

"Why, that, you know, is to— well, they always do that."

"Everybody?"

"Why, yes, everybody. Do you remember what I wrote on your slate?"

"Yes."

"What was it?"

"I won't tell you."

"Shall I tell *you*?"

"Yes, yes—but some other time. Tomorrow."

"Oh, now, Becky. Now. I'll whisper it in your ear."

Tom took her silence for consent, passed his arm around her waist, and whispered the words softly, with his mouth close to her ear. Then he added:

"Now you whisper it to me, just the same way."

She turned to him and said:

"Tom, you look away so you can't see, and then I will. But you must never tell anyone—promise? You won't, will you?"

"No. Indeed I won't, Becky."

He turned his face away, and she bent over his head until her plaited blond tails fell about him and her breath was warm in his ear. "I—love—you!"

Tom was in heaven.

"Now, Becky, it's all done—all over but the kiss. Don't be afraid of that. It won't be anything at all."

She tensed up and he waited, and by and by she gave up and relaxed. Tom kissed her sweet lips, and they both closed their eyes for the event.

"Now it's all done, Becky. And after this, you know, you ain't ever to like anyone but me, and you ain't ever to marry anyone but me. Never, ever, forever. Will you?"

"No. I'll never love anybody but you, Tom, and I'll never marry anybody but you—and you won't marry anyone but me, either."

"Why, of course! That's part of it. When we're going home, you're to walk with me, and at parties, you choose me and I choose you, because that's the way you do when you're engaged."

"I've never heard of any of this before. This is such a nice practice."

"Oh, it's the best. Why, me and Amy Lawrence—"

Her eyes told Tom he had made a serious mistake, and he stopped, confused.

"Oh, Tom! I'm not the first girl you've been engaged to!"

She began to cry. Tom said:

"Oh, don't cry, Becky. I don't care for her no more."

"Yes you do, Tom. Yes you do."

Tom tried to put his arm around her and comfort her, but she pushed him away and turned her face to the wall, still crying. Tom tried again, and was repulsed again. Then he began to feel badly, fearing he was in the wrong. She stood sobbing, her head against the wall. Tom's heart broke. He said:

"Becky—I—I don't care for anybody but you."

There was no reply. Just more sobs.

"Please," he implored her. "Won't you say somethin'?"

More sobs. She would not be reasoned with.

Tom walked out of the school and plodded toward home, not seeing the road or the sky, not feeling the wind, and not hearing the call of the birds. Presently, Becky ran to the door, but Tom was no longer in sight. Her footsteps seemed sinister and empty in the deserted schoolhouse and she called out:

"Tom! Come back, Tom!"

She listened, but there was no answer. Once again, she had no companion but silence and loneliness. She went outside and sat down to cry in old Mr. Branson's chair, and she cried until she could cry no more. Then, like Tom, she walked home, numb and oblivious to the growing streaks of red in the sky, and to any Zum that might have been crashing aimlessly through the gathering dark.

8

Deciding on a Vocational Path

Tom went back and forth through the lanes and fell into a moody jog. He crossed a small creek three times, because of a prevailing superstition that to cross water baffled pursuit. Half an hour later he was in back of the Douglas mansion on the highest point of the village. There was a man he didn't recognize in one of the guard towers, and he was smoking a cigarette, watching Tom's progress, and when Tom took off his hat and waved, the man nodded his head in response. From his bored countenance, Tom knew there was no trouble about. Not even a zephyr stirred. The heat of the day had even stilled the song of the birds, and nature lay in a trance that was broken by no sound but the occasional far-off hammering of a woodpecker, and this seemed to intensify the pervasive silence and make his loneliness more profound. His soul was steeped in melancholy. He sat on the bank of a small creek with his elbows on his knees and his chin in his hands, meditating.

It seemed to him that life was a bit of trouble, at best, and he more than half envied Jimmy Hodges, so lately released. Jimmy was a boy Tom's age, and he had taken a shortcut late one afternoon on the way home from a successful squirrel hunt. He had bagged three fat squirrels, no small accomplishment, and couldn't wait to hoist them above his head in triumph as he entered his home. There were Zum roaming around, though, and looping around one to avoid confrontation, he promptly came upon another. He yanked himself free from the monster's grasp and discharged his weapon—to no avail—and panicked, dropping his squirrels and running deeper into the forest. He ran off the edge of a small cliff, then pitched forward, landing awkwardly and breaking his neck. Tom thought it must be very peaceful to lie and slumber, forever and ever, with the wind whispering through the trees and caressing the grass over the grave, with nothing left to bother and grieve over.

Jimmy was never subsequently invaded by the Zum, a thing so curious that specialists from several counties over were called in to study the phenomenon, postponing the funeral for several days. They came to the conclusion that the severity of the injuries had somehow halted the inevitable process, and they would have enjoyed continuing to poke and measure and experiment on the poor boy, but the parents put an end to it.

It was quite a funeral. There were trifles and lemonade

for the children, and platters of food—squirrel included—
for whoever felt hungry. Jimmy's funeral and subsequent
wake had been the most popular event of the summer, and
well attended, but when Tom mentioned this to his aunt
Polly, she glared at him horribly and told him to keep the
thought to himself.

If Tom only had a cleaner Sunday school record, he would
be willing to go and be done with it all. Now as to the girl—
what had he done? Nothing. He had meant the very best in
the world, and been treated like a dog—like a stray dog. She
would be sorry some day—maybe when it was too late. Ah. If
he could only die *temporarily*.

Tom presently began to drift into the concerns of this
life again. What if he went away and disappeared mysteriously? What if he went away—ever so far away, into the
countries beyond the sea—and never came back at all!
Aunt Polly would mourn his loss forever, and blame herself
for everything. How would Becky feel? The idea of being a
clown now recurred to him, and the very idea was an of-
fense. No, he would travel overseas and be a soldier, and return years later, all warworn and illustrious. Better yet, he
would be a hunter of Zum, with long braided hair, hatchets
hanging bloody and uncleaned from a leather belt, a number of guns slung over his shoulder, notches in every gun,
a sash of Zum pelts or scalps if a person did such a thing.

But he thought of something even gaudier than this. He
would be a pirate! That was it! Now his future lay before
him, filled with unimaginable treasure. How glorious it
would be to plow the dancing sea in his long, black-hulled

ship, the *Spirit of the Storm,* with his grisly flag flying at the
fore. And at the zenith of his fame he would suddenly appear
at the old village and stalk into church, brown and weather-
beaten, in his black velvet doublet, his great jackboots, his
crimson sash, his belt bristling with horse pistols, a cutlass at
his side, and hear with ecstasy the whisperings, "It's Tom
Sawyer the pirate! Black Avenger of the Spanish Main!"

Yes, then, it was settled. His career was determined. He
would run away from home and enter upon it. He would
start that very morning. He would have to get ready.

Just then the blast of a toy tin trumpet came faintly
down the green aisles of the forest. Tom flung off his jacket
and trousers, turned his suspenders into a belt, raked away
some brush behind a rotten log—disclosing a rude bow and
arrow, a wooden sword and tin trumpet—and in a moment
seized these things and bounded away, barelegged, his shirt
fluttering. He stopped under a great elm, blew an answer-
ing blast from the horn, and began to tiptoe and look war-
ily about. He said cautiously—to an imaginary company:

"Hold, my merry men! Keep hid till I blow."

Now appeared Joe Harper, as airily clad and elaborately
armed as Tom. Tom called out to him:

"Hold! Who comes here into the Sherwood without my
pass?"

"Guy of Guisborne wants no man's pass. Who art thou
that—that—"

"Dares to hold such language," said Tom, prompting Joe,
for they were both reciting from the same adventure book
by memory.

"Who art thou who dares to hold such language?"

"I, indeed! I am Robin Hood, as thy miserable carcass shall soon know!"

"Thou are that famous outlaw? Have at thee!"

They took their lath swords, dumping the other props on the ground, struck a fencing attitude, and began brave, careful combat. Presently Tom said:

"Now that you've the hang of it, go it lively!"

So they "went it lively," panting and perspiring with the work. By and by, Tom shouted:

"Fall! Fall! Why don't you fall?"

"Hah! Why don't you fall? You're getting the worst of it."

"Why, Joe, I can't fall. That ain't the way it is in the book. The book says, 'Then with one backhanded stroke he slew poor Guy of Guisborne.' You're to turn around and let me hit you in the back."

There was no arguing with the authorities, so Joe turned, received the modest whack, and fell. Tom stood over him and recited an elegant monologue over the fallen villain, when suddenly Joe lurched back to his feet.

"Hey!" Tom began. "Hey!" But Joe growled and wrestled Tom to the ground. "Hey! I wasn't finished!"

Joe worked Tom over onto his stomach and began raining his head with handfuls of dirt and grass and dead leaves. Tom sputtered indignantly and said: "You're not playing fair, Joe. You're dead, Sir Guy!"

Joe cackled triumphantly. "Aha! Evil Guy Guisborne, struck down by Robin Hood! He falls and rises again as the double evil *dead* Guy Guisborne! Guy the Zum!

"Without regret, he begins to eat the back and neck muscles of Robin of Locksley. Oh, nom nom nom! The hero is powerless now to defeat me!"

Tom got free and sprang to his feet.

"Then I come back too! The undead Robin Hood! A hero to the poor, and a terror to all living creatures! Okay, let's try it again." The boys fell to wrestling, eating each other's flesh, tearing the limbs off the other and ripping each other's eyes out. They did this until they were exhausted.

Afterward, they jumped into the little creek to cool themselves off, dried themselves, re-hid their accouterments, and disappeared again in the forest going in different directions. They had never extended their game in such a way before, and it was thrilling in ways they scarcely understood. They would have to do it again.

9

Grave Subjects Are Introduced

At half past nine that night, Aunt Polly bolted the door, made sure all the downstairs windows were closed and securely shuttered, and checked to make sure her weapons were ready behind the doors of various rooms. The axe handle, as always, she kept with her, and used it as a prodding tool to move Tom and Sid toward bed. Sid said his prayers and was soon asleep. Tom lay awake in restless impatience. For a while, he heard Polly humming tunelessly in her room as she prepared herself for bed, and shortly thereafter it was quiet, and the whole house was asleep—except for Tom. When it seemed to him that it must be nearly daybreak, he heard the clock on the first floor strike ten! This was despair. He would have thrashed and fidgeted in bed to shake off this feeling, but was afraid of waking Sid. So he lay still and stared into the dark. Everything was oppressively still. By

and by, out of the stillness, little, inconsequential noises began to emphasize themselves. A dog outside sighed and
chewed itself vigorously for fleas. The ticking of the downstairs clock began to bring itself into notice. Old beams
began to creak mysteriously. The stairs creaked faintly, as
though a slow, patient spirit were slowly mounting the
stairs. A measured, muffled snore issued from Aunt Polly's
chamber.

A cricket, somewhere in the room, began to chirp. Some
other insect in the wall next to Tom's bed began to scritch
and tick. It meant that someone's days were numbered.
Then the howl of a far-off dog rose in the night air—
probably some loyal dog sensing the movement of neighborhood varmints—and another faint howl answered it. In
spite of himself, Tom began to doze, and when the clock
struck eleven, he did not hear it. And then it came, mingling
with uneasy, half-formed dreams, a bird calling, somewhere
just outside his window.

It was no ordinary bird.

"Coo-kerroo. Coo-kerroo. Tom!" the bird sang urgently.
"Coo-kerroo." There was no movement from Tom's window.

"Tom! Wake up! Coo-kerroo!"

Tom woke in an instant, and for a moment was standing
in both worlds, the world of the living and the world of the
sleeping. Pulling himself out of sleep, he dressed and crawled
out the window. He cawed like a blue jay once or twice as he
went. In seconds, he was down to the ground. Huckleberry
Finn was there, standing with his magical dead cat. The boys

moved off and disappeared in the gloom. At the end of a half hour, they were wading through the tall, unkempt grass at the graveyard.

It was a typical graveyard of the time. It sat on the edge of a small hill, about a mile and a half outside the village. It had a useless wooden fence around it, originally installed to make it seem pleasant and quaint, but it had been broken and repaired several times since the beginning of all the troubles with the Zum. Several of them had resurrected themselves from pine boxes beneath the ground, clawing their way back to the surface, and thus freed themselves. They knew nothing of gates, but smashed their way through whatever barrier was in front of them. At first the fence was fixed immediately and soon after repainted. But it had happened often enough that the people of the village gradually stopped the repair and simply cleaned up the splintered boards or carted them away for firewood. Things were not as they had once been, and the living were powerless to bring the old ways back.

Grass and weeds grew unchallenged over the whole cemetery, the familiar chicory growing to three feet tall, its soft blue flowers adding a touch of beauty. But the graveyard was not the quiet, pretty, tranquil place it had once been. It was mostly abandoned, and no longer did groups of church women come to clean the area, right the wooden tombstones, and knock down the weeds. No, those days were over. People who wanted to remember their loved ones a bit more fondly were now more apt to put them somewhere on their own property. All the older graves were sunken in, the bodies gone to worm and dust, and there was no threat from these sites. Cremation would have been a neat solution, and indeed it was more commonplace in the larger cities, but in rural areas a funeral pyre seemed to attract the Zum, as moths are attracted to a flame. It distracted and annoyed the grieving survivors, and gave them no solace. As a result, it was rarely done.

There was not a tombstone left standing in the place, all of them having been knocked down by animals, the elements, or wandering Zum. "Sacred to the Memory of" So-and-so had been painted on them once, but the colors had all faded and could no longer be read.

A faint wind moaned through the trees, and Tom feared it was the spirits of the dead, come to complain about being disturbed. Tom and Huck both listened for the accompanying snap of twigs or the rustling of branches, but none came. Angry spirits could be endured; the Zum would have to be avoided. They found the sharp new heap they were looking for and ensconced themselves in the protection of three giant elms that grew within a few feet of the grave.

They waited in silence for what seemed to be a long time. The hooting of a distant owl was the only noise that cut through the dead silence. Tom's reflections grew oppressive, and he said in a whisper:

"Hucky, do you believe the dead people mind for us to be here? Not the Zum, the dead."

Huckleberry whispered:

"I wish't I knowed. It's awful peculiar here, ain't it?"

"It surely is."

There was a considerable pause, then Tom whispered:

"Say, Huck—do you suppose Hoss Williams hears us talking?"

"O'course he does. Least his spirit does."

Hoss Williams had worked in the livery and lived by himself. He had fallen off a haymow and onto a pitchfork. He was relatively penniless, relatively friendless, and the quick and expedient funeral consisted of a few men taking off their hats, saying a brief prayer, wrapping him in several layers of canvas, and binding him again and again with a length of good thick rope. That and five feet of poor, compacted soil was deemed enough to secure him within the earth.

Tom, after a pause:

"I wish I'd said Mister Williams. But I never meant him any harm. Everyone called him Hoss."

"A body cain't be too careful how you talk about these dead people, Tom."

This was a damper, and the conversation died again.

Presently, Tom seized his comrade's arms and said:

"Sh!"

"What is it, Tom?" And the two boys clung together with beating hearts, ready to bolt in the opposite direction of the noise Tom heard.

"Shh! There 'tis again! Hear it?"

"Lord, Tom. They're comin'. They're comin' sure. What'll we do?" Suddenly the magical dead cat in his arms seemed woefully inadequate.

"I dunno. Think they'll see us?"

There was no good answer for that, as the Zum did not

appear to be dependent on sight. More often than not, their eye sockets were empty, hollow, and black.

"Oh, don't be afraid. I don't think they'll bother us. If we keep perfectly still, maybe they won't notice us at all."

"I'll try, Tom, but Lord, I'm all of a shiver."

The boys huddled together and scarcely breathed. A muffled sound of voices floated up from the far end of the graveyard. Presently, Huckleberry whimpered with a shudder:

"It's them, sure enough. Three of 'em! Lordy, Tom, we're goners. Can you pray for me?"

"Sh!"

"What is it, Tom?"

Tom had noticed it a moment earlier. The Zum did not speak. They grunted and gurgled and moaned and often howled like tormented demons, but they did not speak. It was a talent somehow denied them.

"They're humans!" Tom whispered. "One of 'em is, anyway. One of 'em's old Muff Potter. Listen! And don't you stir nor budge. Muff's not sharp enough to notice us, even if he's sober, and he ain't never is."

"All right, I'll keep still," Huck replied.

"Say, Huck, I know another one o' them voices. It's Injun Joe!"

"That's so, Tom—that murderin' half-breed! I'd rather they was devils. What kin they be up to?"

The two stopped talking completely, for the three men had reached the grave and stood within a few feet of the boys' hiding place.

"Here it is," said the third voice. The owner of it held a lantern up and revealed the face of young Dr. Robinson. He had attended medical school back east only a few years earlier, and come back to town to battle human suffering. He had learned about medicines and tinctures and poultices, and how to set broken limbs, but nothing in medical school had prepared him for the Zum. Now he felt like he was spending the shank of his days scurrying from house to house, severing the heads of the recently deceased. It insulted his abilities, and like many other doctors around the world, he quietly resolved to find out more about this accursed condition in order to defeat it. To this end, he became a grave robber, so this was not his first late-night excursion into the cemetery.

Potter and Injun Joe were carting a handbarrow with a rope and a couple of shovels on it. They cast down their load and began to open up the grave. The doctor put the lantern at the head of the grave and sat against one of the elm trees. He was so close the boys could have touched him.

"Hurry, men!" he said in a low voice. "Any Zum comes out of the darkness and we're through here."

Injun Joe laughed bitterly. "What's the difference? We give 'em a bash on the head and that will be that. I'm not worried about them."

For some time there was no noise but the grating sound of the shovels as they discharged their weight of mold and gravel. It was tedious work. Finally, a spade hit the wrapped and bound figure, and within another minute they hoisted it out of the ground. They cut a section of the canvas and exposed the pallid face. Its eyes were open, and as soon as the cloth fell away, it began to moan horribly.

Potter took out the large spring-knife and prepared to sever the head, saying:

"I'm ready here, Sawbones. Now you just come through with another five, and off it comes. Another five, or on it stays."

"That's the talk!" said Injun Joe.

"Look here, what does this mean? I've already paid the both of you for this."

Injun Joe stood in front of the doctor.

"Yeah, and you've done more than that. Five years ago, you drove me from your father's kitchen table one night, when I came in to ask for somethin' to eat. You said I warn't there for any good; and then I swore I'd get even with you if it took a hundred years. Did you think I'd forget? The native blood what's in me ain't for nothin'. Now I've got you, and you've got to settle!"

The bound and helpless Zum that had once been Hoss Williams suddenly let out a horrible moan, and the doctor took the opportunity to strike out and bring Joe to the ground with a solid fist. Potter dropped the knife and exclaimed:

"Here now, you've hit my pard!" and the next moment the two were struggling with might and main, trampling the grass and tearing the ground with their heels. Through it all, Hoss Williams continued to bay and howl. Injun Joe sprang to his feet, his eyes flashing with passion, and he snatched up Potter's knife, circling the combatants, waiting for an opportunity.

All at once Potter fell backward over the bound Zum, and the doctor picked up one of the heavy, abandoned wooden tombstones and knocked Potter in the head with it. In the same instant, Joe saw his opportunity and drove the knife to the hilt in the young man's breast. The doctor reeled and fell on top of Potter, flooding him with his blood, and in the same moment, the moon went behind the clouds and the two frightened boys went speeding away in the dark.

When the moon emerged again, Joe was standing over the three forms, contemplating them. The doctor moaned, once, inarticulately, curiously distinct from the noises coming from the Zum, gave a last gasp, and was still. Joe muttered:

"That score is settled—damn you."

Then he robbed the doctor's body. After this, he put the fatal knife in Potter's open right hand and sat down on a mound of earth, eyeing both his companion and the moaning Zum. Three to five minutes passed, and then Potter began to stir and call out. His hand closed upon the knife; he raised it, glanced at it, and let it fall back to the earth. Then he sat up, pushing the body off him, and gazed about, confused. His eyes met Joe's.

"Lord, what is this, Joe?" he asked.

"It's a dirty business," Joe said, not moving. "You've killed him."

"I never did it!"

"Look here. That sort of talk won't wash. You surely did."

Potter trembled and grew white.

"I shouldn't 'a' drunk tonight. I had no business. I'm all in a muddle here; can't recollect hardly any of it. Tell me, Joe, honest now—did I do it? Upon my soul and honor, I never meant to. Oh, Joe, it's awful, tell me how it went—him so young and promising."

"Why, you two started scuffling, and you fell over Hoss Williams there. The doc fetched you one with one of them boards and you went flat. Then up you came, knife in your hand, and jammed it into him, just as he gave you another lick. And here you've laid, as dead as a wedge until now—deader'n old Hoss there."

"Oh, I didn't know what I was doin', Joe. May I die this minute if I did. It was all on account of the whiskey, and the excitement, and that damn noise-makin' Zum. I've fought before, but never with weapons. Joe, you ain't gonna tell? Say you won't, Joe. I always liked you, and stood up for you, too. You won't tell, will you?" And the poor creature began to sob with remorse.

"Now, you've always been fair and square with me, Muff Potter, and I won't go back on you. There now, that's as far as a man can say. Ol' Hoss here won't say a word, either, will ya, Hoss? That's two fer two!"

"Oh Joe, you're an angel. An angel!" And Potter began to sob anew.

"Come on, that's enough of that. There ain't any time for blubberin'. You go off yonder that way, and I'll go off this. Move now, and be careful not to leave a track."

Potter started off at a jog that quickly increased to a run.

Joe stood and watched him run into the darkness. He muttered:

"If he's as much stunned with the lick and the rum as he had the look of being, he won't be thinking of the knife till he's gone so far he'll be afraid to come back after it himself—chicken heart!"

Two or three minutes later the murdered man, the moaning, bound corpse, and the open grave were under no inspection but the moon's. The undead figure stared unseeing at the full moon and continued to moan and thrash, but to little effect. Everything else went silent.

10

Dire Circumstances

The two boys flew on and on toward the village, speechless with horror. They glanced backward over their shoulders from time to time, apprehensively, as if they feared something might be following them. Every branch blocking their path seemed to be the awful, clutching arms of a Zum, and made them catch their breath. As they sped by some of the outlying cottages that lay near the village, the barking of aroused watchdogs seemed to give wings to their feet.

"If we can only get to the tannery!" Tom gasped, in short breath. "I can't stand it much longer!"

Huckleberry's panting was his only reply. At last, they burst through the door of the deserted building and fell gratefully and near exhaustion into the shadows therein. By and by, their pulses slowed and Tom whispered:

"Huckleberry, what do you reckon'll come of this?"

"If Doc Robinson dies, I reckon a hanging'll come of it."

"You think?"

"I know it, Tom."

"Who'll tell? You and me?"

Huckleberry thought about it. "Doesn't seem like a good idea in my mind. S'pose somethin' happened and Joe got off. Why, he'd come after us and kill us, sooner or later, just like he laid for the doc."

"I was thinkin' that, too."

"If anybody tells, let Muff Potter do it. He's fool enough."

Tom said nothing, thinking to himself. And then it came to him.

"Huck, Muff Potter don't *know* it. How can he tell?"

"Why don't he know it?"

"Because he just took that whack when ol' Joe done it. I don't believe he was aware of anything."

"By hokey, that's so, Tom."

"And besides—maybe that whack he took done *him* in, too!"

"No, 'tain't likely. He had liquor in him—a whole bunch of it. When Pap's full, you could belt him over the head with a church and it wouldn't faze him. So it's probably the same with Potter. If a man was dead sober, I reckon that whack might fetch him. Ah, I dunno."

After another reflective silence, Tom said:

"Hucky, you sure you can keep mum?"

"Tom, we got to. You *know* that. Joe wouldn't have no more trouble drownin' us than a couple of cats, if we was to squeak about this. Look-a-here, Tom, let's swear to each other—swear to keep mum."

"I'm agreed. Shall we just hold up our hands and say an oath?"

"No, no. That wouldn't do for this. They orter be writin' about a big thing like this. And blood to boot."

Tom's whole being applauded this idea. It was deep, and dark, and terrible; the hour, the circumstances, and the surroundings. The moaning and horrible noises coming from what had been Hoss Williams were bad enough. The murder of Doc Robinson was somehow much worse, unimaginable, almost unspeakable. He picked up a clean pine shingle that lay in the moonlight, took the stub of a carpenter's pencil from his pocket, and wrote the following:

Huck Finn and Tom Sawyer swear they will
keep mum about this and wish they
be torn to pieces by the dead
if they ever tell.

Huckleberry was filled with admiration for Tom's facility in writing. Then each boy pricked the ball of his thumb with a pin and squeezed out several drops of blood, and put their thumbprints on the document. They buried the pine shingle close to the wall, and recited some suitable, dismal incantations on the burial site.

A figure crept ungracefully through a break in the ruined building, but they did not notice it. The boys continued to whisper for some time, recounting the story again and again as if they themselves did not actually believe what they had just witnessed. Presently a dog set up a long, guttural moan outside—just ten feet from them. The boys jumped to their feet in an agony of fright.

"What is it?" gasped Huckleberry.

"I dunno—peep through the crack. Quick!"

"No, you, Tom!"

"I can't—it's too awful! There 'tis again!"

Again the dog let out a burbling, dreadful moan.

Tom looked through the crack in the wall.

"It's Harbison's ol' dog, Buddy."

The dog let out another horrible moan. The boys' hearts sank some more.

"I don't know about that. That dog is soundin' somethin' mighty strange!" Huckleberry whispered.

Tom put a closer eye to the crack. His whisper was barely audible when he said:

"Oh, Huck. It's turned Zum! 'Tain't no natural dog at all!"

"Lemme see!" Huck peered through the same crack.

"I never heard of no dog goin' Zum, Tom. Never. No other animals, either. That cat I had never turned—he jus' stayed dead. What do you reckon? Mebbe it's just the dog's taken sick."

"Take a good look at him," Tom said. "His hair fallin' out all over, there's dried blood stuck everywhere on his back. I think some of his bones are pokin' through. And I can smell him from here. He smells dead."

"Lordy, I think you're right. I never saw me a live dog that looked that poorly. You suppose he means to eat us?"

"He ain't up to no good, that's for certain."

Huckleberry looked around the floor of the tannery until he came on a decent-sized rock.

"What're you doin', Huck?"

"Gonna scare him outta here." He opened the door of the tannery and hurled the rock at the dog's head. It bounced off his chest but drew no response from the dog whatsoever. Its chest seemed to writhe like a spaded worm, but they realized it was a movement caused by maggots.

"Yep," Huck said, feeling sick to his stomach. "That's a Zum thing."

Soon, the dog loped off into the night, but in moments, Tom again pricked up his ears.

"Sh! Now what's that noise?"

"Sounds like—like hogs gruntin'. No—it's somebody snorin', Tom. Sounds so, anyways. Pap used to sleep here sometimes, 'long with the hogs. Been awhile for him, though."

The spirit of adventure rose in the boys' souls once more, and they pushed the thought of the dog out of their minds and moved toward the sound. When they were close enough, Tom stopped and whispered:

"Hucky, come foller right behind me."

"I don't like to much, Tom. S'pose it's Injun Joe!"

Tom quaked. But the temptation rose up in them and they agreed to look, with the clear understanding that they would withdraw if the snoring stopped. When they came to within a few feet of the snorer, Tom stepped on a stick, and it broke with a sharp snap. The man moaned, writhed a little, and his face came into the moonlight.

It was Muff Potter. The boys' hearts stood still, and their hopes too, when the man moved, but their fears passed away. Muff was gone, passed out, oblivious to worldly concern. They tiptoed out, through a broken weather board, and stopped some distance away to exchange parting words. Faintly, on the wind, they could still hear the Zum dog's watery moaning, but the sound came from afar. The dog was moving away. It was strange, most powerfully strange, but it came on a night filled with strange.

When Tom crawled into his bedroom window, the night was almost over. The sky was violet, the sun about to come up, and the first birds of the morning were stirring and beginning to make noise. He undressed wearily and fell asleep congratulating himself that no one was aware of his escapade. He was not aware that the gently snoring Sid in the other bed was awake, and had been so for an hour, waiting for Tom's return.

When Tom awoke, Sid was dressed and gone. Sunlight was streaming in the windows, and there was a late sense to the day. Why had he not been called down to breakfast? The thought filled him with unease. Within five minutes he was dressed and downstairs, feeling sore and drowsy. There was no voice of rebuke, but there were averted eyes, and a silence that struck a chill into his heart. He sat down and tried to appear gay and lighthearted, but he aroused no smiles, no response, and he lapsed into silence.

After breakfast, his aunt took him aside, and Tom almost brightened in the hopes that he was going to be flogged, but it was not so. His aunt wept over him and asked how he could break her old heart so, and what was she to do if he wouldn't listen to her—nail him into bed each night? It was no use to even try anymore. This was worse than a thousand whippings, and Tom's heart was now as sore as his body. He too cried, and pleaded for forgiveness, promising to reform, but she merely shook her head and he received his dismissal.

He moped to school gloomy and sad, and took his flogging there along with Joe Harper, for playing hooky the day before. He then took his seat and stared at the wall with the air of a man who has reached his limit and can go no farther. He looked at Becky, across the aisle, until he caught her eye, but she too shook her head and refused again to meet his glance. He signaled the girl next to Becky, who yanked on her sleeve and pointed toward Tom, but Becky was resolute and would not even gaze in his general direction.

His heart was broken yet again, and his spirits settled uniformly into a dark torpor.

11

A Killer Is Apprehended

By noon, the whole village was abuzz and electrified with
the ghastly news. An early-morning visitor to the graveyard had heard the grunts and howls of Hoss Williams, investigated, and discovered the murder. The tale flew from
man to man, from group to group, from house to house, until everyone was aware of it. Of course, the schoolmaster
canceled school for the rest of the day; the town would have
thought it odd if he had not.

A gory knife had been found near the murdered man,
and it had been recognized as something belonging to Muff
Potter. And it was said that a belated citizen had come upon
Potter washing himself in the creek close to two in the
morning, and that Potter had at once sneaked off—all very
suspicious, especially the washing, which was not a fixed
habit with Potter. The village was searched thoroughly for

the suspect, but he was not found. Horsemen departed down all the roads in every direction, and the sheriff was confident that his man would be captured by nightfall. Before the crowd grew too much larger, the sheriff quickly ordered a small complement of men to re-bury Hoss Williams, as the noise was a nuisance and a hindrance to his concentration. He also ordered another group of men to prepare Doc Robinson for a brief and expeditious funeral. He had not yet "turned," but he would, undoubtedly, and soon.

All the town began drifting toward the graveyard. Tom's heartache vanished and he joined the procession, not because he was curious, as he was already aware of what he would find there, but because of a powerful, unaccountable fascination that drew him on. Arriving at the dreadful place, he worked his way through the crowd and saw the dismal spectacle. A group of men were grappling with the body of Hoss Williams like it was the body of a freshly caught fish, thrashing in the bottom of a rowboat. Inevitably, they worked him close to the open grave and rolled him in. Their faces were white with effort and obvious distaste, and they quickly filled the hole.

Someone pinched Tom's arm. He turned, and it was Huckleberry. They both glanced around them, wondering if anyone had noticed something suspicious in their mutual glance. But there was too much to take in, too much to see, too much to witness, and everyone was talking to one another—and loudly.

"Poor fellow!"

"Poor doc!"

"This will be a lesson to grave robbers!"

"Muff Potter'll be hung for this if they catch him!"

Tom shivered from head to toe, for his eye fell upon the emotionless face of Injun Joe. At this moment, the crowd began to sway and pull itself in different directions, and voices began to shout: "It's him! It's him! He's comin' through! Comin' through!"

"Who? Who?" answered a number of voices.

"Muff Potter!"

"Hallo! He's stopped—look out, he's turnin'! Don't let him get away!"

People perched in the trees above Tom's head said he wasn't trying to get away—he just looked doubtful and confused.

"What gall!" said a bystander. "He wanted to come back and take a quiet look at his work, I reckon! Didn't expect any company so soon."

The sheriff came through the crowd, leading Muff by the arm. Muff's face was empty, streaked with tears, and he was haggard, showing the fear that was upon him. When he stood before the murdered man—presently being wrapped and bound as Hoss had been—he shook as with a palsy and burst into tears.

"I didn't do it, friends," he sobbed. "Upon my word and honor, I never done it!"

"Who says you did?" shouted an observant voice.

Potter lifted his face and looked about him with a

pathetic hopelessness in his eyes. He saw Injun Joe and exclaimed:

"Oh, Joe, you promised me you'd never——"

The sheriff interrupted him. "Is this your knife?"

Potter would have swooned and fallen to the ground had the men not caught him and eased him down to the weedy earth. Then he said:

"Somethin' told me if I didn't come back and get——" He waved a limp and helpless hand with a vanquished shudder and said: "Tell 'em, Joe, tell 'em—it ain't no use no more."

Then Huckleberry and Tom stood dumb and staring, and heard the stony-hearted liar reel off his fabricated story, and they expected at any moment that the sky would open and there would be a celestial rumbling and God would deliver a bolt of lightning to his head. But when Joe finished and still stood alive and whole, their impulse to move forward and save the poor prisoner's life faded and vanished away, for it was now clear that Joe had sold himself over to Satan, and it would be fatal to meddle with such a power as that.

"Why didn't you leave? What did you come back here for?" someone shouted.

"I couldn't help it," Potter moaned. "I couldn't help it. I wanted to run away, but I couldn't seem to come anywhere but here." And he fell to sobbing again.

Joe repeated his statement, just as calmly, a few minutes later at the inquest, and the boys—noticing the lack of lightning or even thunderclouds—were confirmed in their belief that he had sold himself to the devil. He was now the most terrifying and baleful thing Tom had ever looked upon, and they could not take their eyes from his face. When Tom had thrown a rock at the Zum dog, he'd had a sick feeling that the dog would haunt his nightmares for a time to come. Now he had a much different feeling. The Zum dog had done nothing. Joe had done it all. Both Tom and Huck inwardly resolved to watch him in the future, in the hopes of getting a glimpse of his dread master.

Muff was taken away, the poor doctor hoisted onto a cart and driven off to effect his final rites, and Joe disappeared into the crowd, strolling and chatting with whoever would talk with him without a glance back over his shoulder.

Tom's fearful secret and gnawing conscience destroyed his sleep for the nights to come, and at breakfast one morning, Sid said:

"Tom, you pitch around and talk in your sleep so much you keep me awake half the time."

Tom blanched, and said nothing, staring at his hands.

"It's a bad sign, Tom," said Aunt Polly gravely. "What do you got on your mind?"

"Nothin'. Nothin' I know of."

Sid said: "Last night you said, 'It's blood, it's blood, that's what it is!' You said that over and over. And you said, 'Don't torment me so—I'll tell! I promise, I'll tell!' Tell what? What is it you'll tell?"

Everything was swimming before Tom. Luckily Aunt Polly sighed mightily and came to his relief without knowing it. She said:

"Sho! That dreadful murder. I dream about it almost every night myself."

Mary chimed in and said she had been affected much the same way. Sid seemed satisfied by these statements.

Tom's dreams continued, though, until there was a dreadful uniformity to them. Everyone in the village was dead, or gone. Screams of the dead and dying came from every house. Aunt Polly was nowhere to be found. His house had been ransacked and stood empty, the doors splintered, open, and useless. There was ash in the air and a smell of sulphur, burnt feathers, and rotten meat. Tom had barricaded himself in his bedroom, but he heard faint footsteps walking up the stairs to his room, and he tried to call out to his aunt, to anyone, but could not. The door opened, and the black Zum dog sat there, magically transformed. Its coat was healthy, rich, and shiny. Its eyes were clear and bright. It was on a short leash, and holding the leash, walking confidently into the room, was Injun Joe. Most of the flesh on his face was gone, and his teeth showed like an insane grin. Maggots and flies crawled over his flesh, and he leaned over and said to the dog: "Good boy! Good boy!" and the dog warmed to his praise and began licking his face. This was usually where Tom woke up.

Every day or so at this time of sorrow, Tom went to the little grated jail window and took such small comforts through to the "murderer" as he could put his hand on. Usually, it would be an apple, a piece of fruit, a lump of sugar, a stolen warm cookie. The jail was a small brick den that stood in a marsh near the edge of town, and no guards were afforded to it. Muff was the only inhabitant. These daily offerings greatly helped Tom to ease his conscience.

The village had a strong desire to tar and feather Joe for his part in the crime, but so formidable was his character that no one could be found to take a lead in the matter, so it was dropped. He had been careful to begin both of his inquest statements with the fight, without commenting or confessing to his part in the grave robbery that preceeded it; it was therefore deemed wisest not to try that case in the courts at present. Perhaps Joe invaded no other dreams in the village, but everyone knew the kind of person he was, and therefore had no illusions as to what he was capable of should he set his mind to it.

So they left Joe alone.

12

The Cat and the Effective Tonic

A person can dwell on the same events for only a limited time before he grows weary of them in his mind. This is what happened to Tom. Other worldly matters began to crowd into his head and interest him. Highest on the list was Becky Thatcher, for she had stopped coming to school. In his current state of mind, Tom imagined she might die and be out of his life forever. It was an outrageous thought, but absolutely reasonable. People seemed to die; it was the nature of things. They died and were changed forever. Nothing brought them back—at least the way you remembered them. There was no magical elixir, no effective incantations involving a friend's dead cat. It was just something that happened. The spark of life vanished. Tom dwelled extensively on this harsh truth, and his aunt grew deeply concerned.

She began to try all manner of remedies on him. Aunt Polly had been a volunteer at the small, one-room library, and she had a particular interest as far as reading materials—the health of the physical body. She read everything on the topic, and when something fresh on this subject came in the door, in tract or pamphlet or bound copy of a book, she was ready to reproduce the experiments on herself and her loved ones.

She was interested in medicine and remedies to illness and special healing powers, and believed if someone had taken the time to write down such a thing, it was not only true, but reproducible. She read about a thing and was immediately in a fever to try the same thing right away, if not on herself, then on someone else. She read periodicals on the correct way to breathe, which direction was the most advantageous to sleep in, how to wake up, what to eat, what to drink, how much exercise to take, what frame of mind her head should be in, what kind of clothes to wear, what color her clothing should be, and the benefit of a positive attitude. She ground the roots of common weeds, added herbs, camphor, and a dollop of whiskey from a bottle she kept underneath the kitchen sink, and applied it behind her ears as a supposed powerful Zum repellent. Her belief was that *some* of it had to work, and the rest would at least not harm her.

She was looking for an edge against a stacked deck. The dead rose up to strike down the living, and no reason for it had ever been given, other than the nonmedical one subscribed to by the church. The smartest minds in the world could not come up with a good explanation, so if the curative powers of orange bonnets, lemon juice, laughter, or a certain type of wood smoke promised some kind of relief, she was ready to be relieved. She was as simple-hearted and honest as the day was long, and so she was an easy victim. She gathered together her quack periodicals, and her quack medicines, and at least it was a kind of belief and a moving forward. It was all she had.

The latest remedy she had read about was the water treatment, and it insinuated that the treatment itself might even have some benefits with the recently dead, though research in this area had not yet been funded. Tom's whole condition was a windfall for her. She had him out at daybreak every morning, stood him out in front of the woodshed, and doused him with a deluge of cold water. Then she scrubbed him down with a rough, dry towel, rolled him in a wet sheet, and put him under blankets till he sweated his soul clean.

The boy, however, grew more and more melancholy, and detached. She added hot baths, sitz baths, shower baths, and plunges. The boy remained as dismal as ever. She began to complement the water cure with an oatmeal diet and blister patches. She calculated his capacity for treatment as she would a jug, and filled him up every day with cure-alls.

Tom became indifferent to this torture. Perhaps, he thought, it was something he deserved. Perhaps it might make him whole again. Then she heard of Painkiller for the first time. The flyer said it rejuvenated the sick and made the healthy healthier. She ordered a quantity at once. When it was received, she tasted it, and was filled with a new hope.

It was simply fire in liquid form. She dropped all the other remedies and pinned her hopes on Painkiller.

She gave Tom a teaspoonful and waited anxiously for the result. Her troubles were instantly at rest, her soul at peace again, for his "indifference" was broken up. The boy could not have shown a heartier interest in life if she had lit a fire underneath him.

Tom didn't enjoy the medicine, but the bitterness of the liquor woke him up. He had been a test subject for Aunt Polly too long, and sought an escape. He immediately hit on the idea of pretending to be fond of Painkiller, and asked for it constantly. This turnaround was exactly the miracle Polly had been waiting for, and she gave Tom a bottle at a time. He would take the bottle upstairs to his room, pour it out the window, or down into a crack in the floor, then go back to Aunt Polly and ask to be given chores. It was all the proof she needed.

One day Tom was in the act of pouring a bottle out the window when his aunt's yellow cat came into the room, purring, eyeing the teaspoon and begging for a taste. Tom said:

"You don't want any. You really don't."

The cat signified that it did.

"You'd better be sure."

The cat was sure.

"Well then, I'll give you a dose, but if you don't like it, you have no one to blame but yourself. And Aunt Polly."

The cat was agreeable. So Tom pried the cat's mouth open

and poured down a good slug of Painkiller. The cat shot a couple of yards into the air, let out a meow like a summer Fourth of July rocket, and flew down the stairs, spreading chaos and destruction in its wake.

Aunt Polly came up the stairs with her axe handle, thinking that a demon or worse had taken possession of the cat. She went into Tom's room and was astonished to find Tom lying on the floor, doubled over with laughter.

"Tom, what happened with that cat?"

"I don't know," gasped the boy.

"I've never seen a cat act so strange."

"Oh, Aunt Polly—cats always act so when they're having a good time."

"They do, do they?" There was a note of distrust in her voice.

"Yes'm. I believe they do."

"You do?"

"Yes'm."

She peered closer, and too late, Tom caught her drift. The empty bottle and teaspoon lay visible at the foot of the bed. Aunt Polly took the spoon and held it up. Tom winced and dropped his eyes. Polly raised him upright by his ear and cracked his head soundly with her thimble.

"Now, Tom, were you tryin' to kill that cat?"

"No, m'am. I was jus' sharin' what I had."

Aunt Polly felt a sudden pang of remorse. Her eyes watered a bit, and she put her hand on Tom's head and said gently:

"I was meanin' only the best, Tom. I was just tryin' to bring you out of it. You know I meant no harm."

Tom looked up at her and was absolutely sincere.

"I know it, Aunt, and so was I with the cat. It done him good, too. I never seen him get around so good."

"Oh, go 'long with you, Tom, before you do somethin' and aggravate me again. See if you can be a good boy, for once, and there'll be no more of this medicine."

Tom reached school ahead of time. He hung around the gate of the schoolyard instead of playing with his comrades. Presently, Jeff Thatcher came into the schoolyard, and Tom's face lit up. He gazed down the road, then mournfully turned his eyes away. Tom went up to him some minutes later and asked where Becky was, but Jeff just laughed and ran into the playground. Whenever a new frock came into view, Tom's heart leapt, until he saw that it was not the right one. At last the frocks had all arrived, and he entered the schoolhouse and sat down to suffer. Then one final frock passed in at the gate, and Tom's heart gave a great bound. The next second he was at it again, yelling, whooping like an Indian, chasing boys, standing on his head—doing everything he could think of to gain her attention.

But she seemed unconscious of it all; she never looked. Could it be possible that she was unaware that he was there? He took his exploits to her immediate vicinity, came warwhooping around her, and finally wound up totally under Becky's nose—almost knocking her down in the process. She turned away, her nose in the air, and he heard her mutter: "Hmmpf!—" and she stopped herself short. All she said was: "Some people are always showing off."

Tom's cheeks burned. He gathered himself up and skulked off, crushed and in need of a large dose of Painkiller.

13

Off to Be a Pirate

Tom's mind was made up now. He was gloomy and desolate. He was a forsaken, friendless boy, he thought; nobody loved him; when they found out what they had driven him to, they would be sorry, all of them; he had tried to do the right thing and get along, but no one would let him; since nothing would please them more than to be rid of him, let it be so; and let them blame *him* for whatever should happen—and why shouldn't they? What right had he to complain? Oh yes, they had forced him to it at last. There was no other choice.

In all truth, the whole world was in much a similar situation. In the decade since the Zum first made their appearance, everyone had felt their lives grow smaller, and felt themselves being shunted into places with fewer alternatives and bleaker circumstances. Joy and spontaneity in all their forms seemed to be fading from the earth. One woke in the morning and heard the birds singing and chirping outside the window, spirits rose, and then the reality of things settled upon a person like a damp shroud. You no longer just opened the door in the morning with a light heart to go and pick berries from a nearby bush to throw into your oatmeal. At least a prudent person would not. There were consequences to consider, sounds to listen for, circumstances to be aware of. The people of the world were now more or less living in armed encampments and had less to worry about from each other than an intruder who seemed to come from nowhere. In another time, it would have been a golden age of peace, but not now. There was no peace.

The world was much different than it had been. Every action seemed to warrant a subsequent caution. Commerce at first ground to a stop, then continued, haltingly. The arts seemed to vanish, and the songs and popular entertainments were largely those of a decade earlier. Civilization was like a flower bulb that has seen insufficient rainfall. The potential was there for beautiful things, but nothing was going to happen unless the weather changed and it received nourishment. Everything seemed suspended, everything seemed wanting, but wanting for what no one had a real clue.

Tom was soon far down Meadow Lane and he heard the school bell tinkle faintly in his ear. He sobbed now, to think he would never, ever hear that familiar sound again—it was very hard, but it was forced on him. Then the weeping came thick and fast.

At this point he met his soul's sworn comrade, Joe Harper—hard-eyed, and with evidently a great and dismal purpose in his heart. Joe's grandparents had been killed by the Zum in one of the initial onslaughts, his own house had been besieged several times, and his parents no longer put the same premium on education they once did. There were too many other things to occupy their thoughts—survival at the forefront.

Tom, wiping his eyes with his sleeve, began to blubber out something about a resolution to escape from the monotony and oppression of home life by roaming abroad into the great world, never to return; and concluded by hoping Joe would never forget him.

It transpired that this was the identical request that Joe had been coming to make of Tom, and that he had come to hit him up for that purpose. His mother had whipped him for playing outside after dark when a neighbor had cautioned that Zum were about, and it was plain she was tired of him and wished him to go. There was nothing to do but give in to her words. He hoped she would be happy, and never regret driving her boy out into an unfeeling, uncaring world of suffering, death, and the constant threat of the undead.

As the two boys walked along, they made a compact to stand by each other and be brothers and never separate until death released them from their troubles. They also swore to stay by each other after death and dispatch the other in a way so as not to be inviting to the Zum; it was an unsavory thing, but it was a measure of true friendship. Then they began to lay out their plans. Joe was all for being a hermit, living on crusts of bread in a remote cave in some elevated location where he could shower any approaching Zum with rocks and boulders should they appear—eventually to die of grief. After listening to Tom, he conceded that there were some conspicuous advantages in a life of crime, and he consented to be a pirate.

Three miles below St. Petersburg, at a point where the Mississippi was a trifle over a mile wide, there was a long, narrow, wooded island, with a shallow sandbar at the head of it, and this seemed perfect as a rendezvous for their enterprise. It was not inhabited; it lay against an almost unpeopled forest; and there would be no surprises from the undead—for they did not swim so much as they floated aimlessly. They might happen to come to a new place as a bit of flotsam carried by the water, but it would not be intentionally. Also, their voyages could not last too many days, or the birds and fish and creatures of the earth would hasten their deterioration. The Zum did not individually last long under the best conditions. Much more past a few days would be too much—their whole framework would collapse upon itself, and they would lose the ability to stand and move. It was for all these reasons that Jackson's Island was chosen.

Then they hunted up Huckleberry Finn, who promptly joined them, for all occupations were one with him; he was indifferent to the process. They agreed to meet out on a lonely spot on the riverbank two miles above the village at an hour when sound-thinking people were ensconced within their homes—midnight. There was a log raft there which they meant to obtain. Each would bring hooks and lines, additional clothes, and such provisions as he could steal—as became outlaws. And before the afternoon was done, they had all managed to spread the fact that the town would soon be "hearing things" about them. It was all very vague and mysterious, and those who were told were cautioned to "be mum and wait."

About midnight, Tom arrived with a boiled ham and a few odds and ends. It was starlight, and very still. The mighty river lay like an ocean at rest. He listened for a moment and heard no other sounds. Then he gave a low, distinct whistle—a bit like a common wren—and was answered in the same way. A guarded voice said:

"Who goes there?"

"Tom Sawyer, Black Avenger of the Spanish Main. Name yourself."

"Huck Finn the Red-Handed, and Joe Harper, Bane of the Zum Curse." Tom had hammered out their titles earlier in the day.

" 'Tis well. Give the countersign." Two hoarse voices delivered the same awful word simultaneously in the brooding night.

"Blood!"

The Bane of the Zum Curse had brought a side of bacon, and had exhausted himself getting it there. Finn the Red-Handed had stolen a skillet, a pouch of cured leaf tobacco, and had brought a few corncobs to make pipes with. However, none of the other pirates chawed, snuffed, or smoked but himself. The Black Avenger of the Spanish Main produced a number of matches and they shoved off, Tom in command, Huck at the oars, and Joe standing guard at the forward. Tom stood amidships, gloomy of countenance, his arms folded, and he gave the orders in a low, serious whisper:

"Luff, and bring her to the wind!"

"Aye, aye, sir!"

"Steady, steady-y-y!"

"Steady as she goes, sir!"

"Let her go a point!"

"A point it is, sir!"

As the boys steadily and monotonously rode the raft downstream, it was no doubt understood that these orders were given only for style and panache, and were not meant to mean anything in particular.

"Finn!"

"Aye, sir!"

"Keep an eye peeled for them murderous dogs, the Zum! Man the swivel guns and the nine-pounders! We'll see if they have a taste for lead!"

"Aye, sir! Very good!"

Then after some moments of quiet contentment:

"What sails she carryin'?"

"Courses, tops'ils, and flying jib, sir!"

"Aye. Sheets and braces! Now, to it, me hearties!"

"Aye, aye, sir!"

The raft came to the middle of the river, and the boys took turns pulling on the oars. The river was not high, and there was not much current. Hardly a word was said for the next three-quarters of an hour. Now the raft was passing before their town, two or three glittering lights to show where it lay. The nightly bonfire in front of the Douglas estate, high on the hill, illuminated the surrounding guard towers and edifices. Tom stood with his arms folded, looking his last at the scene of his former joys and suffering, and wished that "she" could see him now, facing peril and death, going to his certain doom with a grim smile on his lips. Soon afterward, the raft moved away from town and grounded itself on the sandbar above the island, and the boys beached their craft and waded ashore with their freight. Part of the raft's belongings consisted of an old sail, and they used this as a tent to shelter their provisions. They themselves would sleep in the open air, as became pirates. The Zum? Let them dare.

They built a fire against the side of a great fallen log, twenty to thirty feet from the somber depths of the forest, and then cooked up some bacon in the skillet for dinner, using up half of the corn pone they had brought. It was glorious sport to be free and wild and in the forest of that unexplored island, far from the haunts of others, and they said they would never return to civilization. The fire lit up their faces and threw its ruddy glare upon the trees and foliage and festooning vines.

When the last of the crisp bacon was gone and the last allowance of corn pone was devoured, the boys stretched themselves out on the forest floor, which was mostly a soft bed of pine needles, and were filled with contentment.

"This is just the life for me," said Tom. "You don't have to get up when someone says, and you don't have to go to school, and wash, and study, and take tests that don't mean anything, none of that blame foolishness. A pirate don't have to do *anything*, Joe, but a hermit he has to pray and mope around and not have any fun, being all by himself that way."

"I hadn't thought about it that way," said Joe, "but you're right. I'd a good deal rather stay a pirate, now that I've tried it."

"And hermits, bein' off to themselves, have to be on guard and alert all the time, twenty-four hours a day. Pirates can take turns—me, then you, then me."

Huckleberry took no part in this discussion, being better employed. He had finished gouging out a cob, fitted a weed stem to it, loaded it up with tobacco, and was pressing a hot coal to the charge, blowing out clouds of luxurious smoke. He too was in the full bloom of complete contentment. The other pirates envied him this vice, and secretly resolved to acquire it shortly. Presently, he said:

"What do pirates have to do?"

Tom had the answer all ready. He said:

"Nothin'! They just have themselves a bully time, takin' ships and burnin' them, buryin' money in awful places where there's ghosts and Zum to watch over it, and kill everyone on the ships—make 'em walk the plank! And they wear the bulliest clothes!"

"All gold and silver and diamonds!" said Joe with enthusiasm.

"I reckon I ain't dressed fittin' for a pirate," said Huck with regretful pathos in his voice. "I ain't got none but this."

But the other boys told him that fine clothes would come soon enough, once they had begun their adventures. His poor rags were an excellent starting point, and the effect dramatic.

Gradually, their talk died down and drowsiness began to steal over the eyelids of the future pirates. The pipe dropped from the fingers of the Red-Handed, and he slept the sleep of the conscience-free and weary. The other two had a bit more trouble getting to sleep. They hovered on the verge of sleep, but an intruder came, and would not leave. It was conscience. They began to feel a vague fear that they had done wrong to run away. Then they thought of the stolen provisions and the real torture came. They had purloined sweets and apples scores of times, but this was more than "hooking" things—taking hams and other valuables was plain simple *stealing*, and there was a command against this in the Bible, a book that featured punishment and death in many of the chapters. So they inwardly resolved that as long as they remained in the pirate business, they should not sully the experience with the crime of stealing. Conscience then granted a brief truce, and the boys fell asleep.

Almost immediately, Tom was in the middle of his village, and there was smoke and ash in the air. He was alone, but there were cries and screams all about him. As before, he called out for his aunt Polly, but there was no reply. The streets were empty, and most of the houses were open and had been ransacked. The front door of his house had been ripped off its hinges as if by some awful, malevolent force. It was all just a dream, and he knew what was going to happen next, but seemed powerless to put an end to it. He ran upstairs to his room and hid underneath the covers, and waited for the large, black dog to stand in the doorway and call to his master, who would be standing right behind him.

14

In the Camp of the Pirates

When Tom awoke in the morning, he wondered where he was. He sat up and rubbed his eyes and looked around. Then it all came back to him. It was a cool gray dawn, and there was a tremendous sense of peace and relief in the calm and silence of the woods. Not a leaf stirred; no sound obtruded into the scene. Beaded dewdrops stood upon the grass and leaves. On a newly made web, a fat and dimpled white spider was finishing up on his construction, and had already ensnared a satin-white moth. A thin layer of ashes covered the fire and a thin blue line of smoke rose straight into the air. Joe and Huck were still asleep.

Now, far away in the woods a bird called; another one answered; presently the hammering of a woodpecker was heard. Gradually the cool dim gray of the morning whitened, and just as gradually the sounds of nature multiplied and life

manifested itself. A little green worm came crawling over a
dewy leaf, lifting two-thirds of his body into the air from time
to time and "sniffing around," then proceeding again. And
when the worm approached Tom, he sat as still as a stone; and
when at last it considered for a moment and then came down
on Tom's leg and began a journey over him, his whole heart
was glad—for that meant he was going to have a new suit of
clothes—without a doubt a striking pirate captain's. Now a
procession of ants appeared from nowhere in particular, and
went about their labors; one of them struggled mightily with
a dead spider five times as big as itself in its arms, and lugged
it straight up a tree trunk. A scarlet-speckled ladybug climbed
to the top of a large thistle stalk and took wing. A tumblebug
came next, and Tom touched the creature to see it shut its legs
into its body and pretend to be dead. The birds were fairly ri-
oting by this time. A catbird lit in a tree over Tom's head and
trilled out her imitation of her neighbors in a rapture of en-
joyment; then a jay from high atop a tree swept down, a flash
of blue flame, and stopped on a twig almost within the boy's
reach, cocking his head from side to side and eyeing Tom
with a consuming curiosity; a gray squirrel and a larger fox
came scurrying along, sitting up at intervals and chattering at
the boys, for they had probably never seen a human being
before and were unsure whether to be afraid or not. All of
nature was wide awake now, and long shafts of golden sunlight came down through the dense foliage, and the first few
butterflies came flittering into the scene.

Tom stirred the other two pirates and a few moments
later, they were all stripped, whooping and chasing each

other into the shallow, clear water at the end of the sandbar. They felt no longing for the little village, and figured all of them were still sleeping in their beds. A slight rise in the river overnight had carried off their raft, but this only gratified them, since its going was something like burning the last bridge between them and civilization.

They came back to camp wonderfully refreshed, gladhearted, and ravenous. Soon they had the campfire going again, and went about preparing breakfast. While Joe was slicing the bacon, Tom and Huck went to a promising nook at the riverbank and threw in their lines. Almost immediately, they were rewarded. The bacon was not yet finished cooking when they returned with a string of fish, provisions enough for quite a family. They fried the fish with the bacon grease, and were astounded, for no fish had ever seemed that delicious before. They reflected what a fine sauce open-air sleeping, exercise, bathing, and a large portion of hunger makes.

They lay about in the shade, after breakfast, while Huck had a smoke, and then went off through the woods to explore the rest of their forest. They found plenty of things to be delighted with, but nothing to be astonished at. About every hour, they went back in the water to cool off, and it was close to the middle of the afternoon before they got back to camp.

They were too hungry to fish again, but dined sumptuously upon cold ham, then threw themselves down in the shade to talk. But the talk soon began to drag, and then it died. The boys fell to ruminating. A sort of undefined longing crept over them. Presently, it began to take a dim shape—and it resembled homesickness. Even Huck Finn was dreaming of his doorsteps and empty hogsheads. But they were all ashamed of this weakness, and none was brave enough to speak their thoughts.

For some time, the boys had been dully conscious of a peculiar sound in the distance, just as Tom was always aware of the ticking of the downstairs clock at night without being overly attentive to it. But now the sound became more pronounced. The boys all heard it. There was a silence; then a deep, sullen boom came rumbling out of the distance.

"What is it?" exclaimed Joe, under his breath.

"I wonder," said Tom in a whisper.

" 'Tain't thunder," said Huckleberry in an awed tone.

"Listen!" said Tom. "Just listen!"

They waited for a time that seemed like an age, then heard the same muffled boom come rumbling through the trees.

"Let's go and see."

They sprang to their feet and hurried to the shore closest to town. Peering out behind some bushes, they saw a little steam ferryboat about a mile away, drifting with the current. There were a great many smaller boats in the water, but the boys could not determine what the men in them were doing. Presently a great jet of white smoke burst out from the side of the ferryboat, and the same dull rumble of noise was borne to the boys once more.

"I know what 'tis," exclaimed Tom. "Someone's drownded!"

"That's it!" said Huck. "I seen 'em do the same thing last summer, when Bill Turner got drownded—they'd shoot a cannon over the water, and that makes the bodies come to the top."

"Why's that?" asked Joe.

Huck shrugged his shoulders. "I don't know why it is, but I know that's *why* it is. It brings up the body."

"By gum, I wish we was over there," said Joe.

"Me too," said Huck. "I'd give heaps to know who it is."

Presently a thought flashed through Tom's mind, and he exclaimed:

"Boys, I know who drownded—it's us!"

The boys all agreed, and felt wonderful with this revelation. Here was a glorious triumph; they were missed; they were mourned; hearts were broken on their account; tears were being shed. Shameful memories of unkindnesses to the boys were rising up, and helpless feelings of regret and remorse were being indulged. Best of all, the three boys were undoubtedly the talk of the town and had achieved a dazzling notoriety. This was the best.

As night fell, the ferryboat went back to its accustomed business and the skiffs disappeared. The pirates returned to camp. They were giddy, and woozy with vanity and the illustrious trouble they were creating. They caught fish, cooked dinner and ate it, and then fell to guessing what was going on in the village and what was being said about them. But as the shadows of night closed in on them, Tom had a horrible thought, and shared it.

"This means we're all dead," he said flatly.

The boys had a good laugh. "Drownded!" they shouted. "Deader than doornails!"

"So the next time any of them see us—"

They were all silent for a second.

Huck groaned. "They'll think we've gone over and become Zum."

"And they'll want to stove our heads in with shovels or come at us to lop our heads off with something sharp," Tom continued.

There was no answer to that. The three grew quiet, and it seemed more and more that piracy might be the only option left for them. As the night deepened, Huck began to nod, and thence to snore. Joe followed next. Tom lay on his elbows motionless, watching the other two intently. At last he got up cautiously and went searching around the base of a sycamore, picking up two large sheets of bark. Then he knelt by the fire and painfully wrote something on each one with his carpenter's pencil; one he rolled up and put in his jacket pocket, the other he put in Joe's hat, and removed it to a certain distance from the owner. He also put into that hat certain schoolboy treasures of inestimable value— among them a lump of chalk, an India-rubber ball, three fishhooks, and the kind of milky, translucent, highly prized marble known as a "Zum's eye." Then he tiptoed cautiously among the trees until he felt he was out of their hearing, and straightaway broke into a run in the direction of the sandbar.

15

Tom Visits His Grieving Aunt

A few minutes later Tom was in the water, wading toward the Missouri shore. Before the depth reached his middle he was halfway across; the current would permit no more wading, so he struck out confidently to swim the last hundred yards. He swam quartering upstream, but still was swept downward faster than he had expected. He reached the shore finally, and drifted along till he found a low place to pull himself out. Then he struck through the woods, following the shore, his garments soaked and clinging. Shortly before ten o'clock, he came out into an open place that was before the village, and saw the ferryboat lying in the shadows of the trees and high bank. He stopped because he heard voices—two old-timers who had been hired by the ferryboat owner to keep an eye on things during the night.

They smoked and carved pieces of wood and kept each other awake until dawn.

"Damn foolishness with them children," one of them said, and Tom knew they were talking about him.

"Yep. How can a child get past the age of four or five and not know how to swim—at least, you know, enough to dog-paddle to shore?"

"Be a little more charitable, Charles."

"I could'a taught them young boys myself. I used to swim like a fish when'st I was young."

"Nothin' stoppin' you, Charles. Not a thing in the world."

"No way. Water's too cold. I ain't a young man no more."

"I see, I see."

The conversation died and Tom saw the red embers of their cigarettes as they puffed away in the darkness. He was preparing to move away when the conversation got a little more interesting.

"You see what we got on the upper deck, here, Charles?"

"No, I haven't been. Why not save me the trip and you just tell me."

"The bird, Charles—you ain't seen the bird up there?"

"There's birds restin' on the rails most every day. Most nights, too. What's so special?"

"You ain't seen it?"

"I seen birds. Gulls. Crows. All the time. I know what they look like. Make your point."

The man's voice lowered, conspiratorially. "It's still up there. Big ol' thing. Gull. Walkin' around the deck. But it's dead, don't you know."

"What?"

"Zum. I ain't foolin', neither. The feathers are all fallin' off, the beak is half off, the flesh is comin' off here and there, and it makes a goddawful sound. Not like any bird you've ever seen."

"Maybe it's just sick. That's more likely. Never heard of no seagull Zum. Can it fly?"

"Oh, hell, no. Can't hardly walk. Awful-smellin' thing."

"You're gonna make me walk up them stairs, ain't you."

"What do you think?"

"I think we both have to go take a peek and see what we got here. If this is any kind of prank, I'm too old—"

"It's no prank, Charles. I ain't pranked a man in thirty years. Let's go look. Should we take somethin'?"

The other man gave a grizzled làugh and said:

"The day I need somethin' special to fend off a sick bird—Zum or otherwise—is the day I never hope to see. Let's git."

Tom heard the men clomp slowly up the darkened stairs of the ferryboat and could follow their position by the embers of their smokes. Then he heard the snarl of the gull— a wet, unholy chattering that made his hair stand up.

"I'll be go to hell!" one of the men said.

"Careful, Charles."

"Quiet!" The chattering and clomping continued for a few more seconds, until the men cornered the bird and one of them kicked it overboard. There was no flight left in the gull; it fell, shrieking, into the water, and all was still. The two men came back downstairs.

"Well, I believe I'm awake for the rest of the night."

"Me, too. I never saw such a thing. Care for a nip, Charles?"

"Bless you, you've finally said the right thing! Just a small one."

"Take as much as you like. We're entitled."

At this point, Tom continued onward, until he found himself at the perimeter of his aunt's fence. He went through the gate and looked cautiously in the living room window. There sat Aunt Polly, Sid, Mary, and Joe Harper's mother, grouped together, talking. Tom went to the door and softly lifted the latch. He pushed cautiously and stopped each time it began to creak.

"What makes the candle flicker so?" said Aunt Polly. Tom made his way through the door and disappeared under the dining room table—and just in time.

"Why, you must've left that door open, Sid. Go 'long and shut it, if you please. There's too many dangers about. It should be shut."

Tom lay under the table and slowed his breathing for a time so as not to be noticeable, and then crept to where he could almost touch his aunt's foot.

"But as I was sayin'," continued Aunt Polly, "he warn't bad, so to say—just mischievous. I'd say he were full of the devil, but I don't think I will. He never meant no harm. He was jus' no more responsible than a young colt. He was the best-hearted boy that ever was"—and she began to cry.

"It was the same with my Joe—always full of—" She almost said "the devil" but it seemed to be no commendation, so she said: "—full of life, up to every kind of mischief. Oh, bless me, to think that I went and whipped him for taking that cream, never once recollecting that I throwed it out because it was sour, and now I'll never see him again in this world, that poor, poor abused boy." And Mrs. Harper sobbed as if her heart would break.

"I hope Tom's better off where he is," said Sid, "but if he'd 'a' been a little better in some ways—"

"Sid!" Aunt Polly hissed. Tom could hear the approbation in her voice. "Not a word against Tom, now that he's gone. God'll take care of him, never you trouble yourself. Oh, Mrs. Harper, I can't give him up! He was such a comfort to me, though he constantly tormented my ol' heart, so!"

"The Lord giveth and the Lord taketh away—oh, it's so hard! Only last week Joe busted a firecracker right under my feet and I knocked him sprawling! Oh, if I was to do it again, I'd hug him and bless him for it!"

"Yes, yes, I know exactly how you feel, Mrs. Harper. No longer than yesterday I gave Tom a crack on the head with my thimble for givin' Painkiller to the cat, and now . . ."

But this memory was too much for the old lady, and she broke down completely. Tom was snuffling now, himself, and he could hear Mary crying and putting in a kind word for him from time to time.

He continued to listen, and gathered that it was conjectured at first that the boys had drownded taking a swim; then the raft had been noticed missing; next, certain children came forward and said that the missing boys had promised that the village should be hearing something about them soon, and it was determined that the lads had gone off on a lark, and would turn up at the next village down the river. But toward noon, the raft had been discovered, lodged awkwardly against the shore close to seven miles from the village, and there were no boys to be found. Hope perished; they must have drownded, or hunger would have driven them home by now. This was Wednesday. If they continued missing until Sunday, all hope would be given over and the funerals would be preached on that morning. Tom shuddered.

Aunt Polly had one more point to make. It was a delicate one, and she continued awkwardly. "If the boys *have* died, and show up in the future as Zum, are you prepared for that, Mrs. Harper?"

Mrs. Harper was silent for only a moment. "Oh, mercy! The thought had come into my head, and I drove it out again. But no, I'm not prepared. I guess I should be."

"Well, if they're found at all at this point, that's a likely outcome. God rest their souls! One way or t'other, we'll have them a decent burial. If they get brought back as Zum, I just don't think I'll be able to look at them."

The two women flung themselves in each other's arms and had a good, consoling cry, and then parted for the night. Mrs. Harper picked up a large, old blunderbuss that she carried in both hands. Inwardly, she was hoping some Zum—and here she meant anyone other than her son—would assault her on the way home. But her brief anger dissolved back into misery and she went out the door sobbing.

Aunt Polly was tender beyond her wont in her good night to Mary and Sid. Sid snuffled a bit, and Mary went off crying with all her might.

Tom had to keep still long after she went to bed, for she kept moaning and sobbing to herself, tossing restlessly and turning over. But at last she was still, only moaning a little in her sleep. The boy came out from his hiding place, crept gradually to her bedside, and stood regarding her. His heart was full of pity for her. He also knew that, if she opened her eyes suddenly in the darkness, it would be the end of him. He took out his sycamore scroll, and thought of placing it next to her candle, but he put it hastily back in his pocket. Then he bent over and kissed his aunt on her faded cheeks, then straightway made his exit, latching the door behind him.

He threaded his way back to the ferry landing, where the men were still talking, and untied a small skiff that was out of their sight. Soon he was rowing quietly upstream. When he had pulled a mile above the village, he landed the skiff on the opposite shore and set off into the woods.

The night was almost over, and it was broad daylight before he found himself in front of his new island home. He rested in the nook of a tree until the sun was well up, then plunged into the water to refresh himself. A little later he paused, dripping, on the threshold of his camp, and heard Joe say:

"No, Tom's true-blue, Huck—he'll come back. He won't desert us. He's up to somethin' or other, I'll give you that. I just wonder what?"

"Well, the things are ours, anyway, ain't they?"

"Pretty near, but not yet, Huck. The note says they are if he ain't back by breakfast."

"Which he is!" exclaimed Tom, stepping into camp with fine dramatic effect.

A sumptuous breakfast of bacon and freshly caught fish was shortly provided, and Tom recounted—and adorned—his adventures. They were a proud and boastful band of heroes when the tale was done. Then Tom hid himself away in the shade to sleep until noon, and the other pirates got ready to fish and explore.

16

Tom Reveals a Secret

After dinner, the boys turned out to hunt for turtle eggs at the sandbar. They went about poking sticks into the sand, and when they found a soft spot, they would get down on their hands and knees and dig with their hands. Sometimes they would take fifty to sixty eggs out of one hole. They were perfectly round white objects the size of a large walnut. The boys had a great fried egg feast that night, and another the next morning.

After breakfast, they went whooping and prancing out on the bar and chased each other around and around, shedding shirts and pants as they went until they were quite naked, and they continued to frolic in the deep, cooler water. The current tripped their legs out from under them and knocked them off their feet, which greatly increased the fun. When they were all exhausted, they would run out of the water and sprawl on the hot, dry sand until they were bone dry, and then they would break for the water and go through the whole process once more. They took turns playing cowboy versus Indian, shooting and scalping each other a hundred times, and when that paled, they turned the game into Zum versus Zum hunter. The Zum hunters were all crack shots, and their opponents got to make bloodcurdling moans and throw sand and mud on their pursuers—that was one of the few advantages about pretending to be a Zum. There were no rules you had to follow, no code of conduct, and any rules or prohibitions that were being observed, you could ignore or change.

They gradually wandered apart, and fell into the doldrums, gazing longingly across the wide river to where the village lay drowsing in the sun. Tom found himself writing "Becky" in the sand with his big toe; he rubbed it out and was angry at himself for this weakness. But he wrote it again, nevertheless; he could not help himself. He erased it a final time and took himself out of further temptation by driving the boys together and joining them.

But Joe's spirits had gone down almost beyond resurrection. He was so homesick he could barely stand the misery of it. Tears lay very near the surface. Huck was melancholy too. Tom was downhearted, but tried not to show it. He said, with a great show of cheerfulness:

"I bet there's been some pirates on this island before, boys. And I bet they've hid treasures about somewheres. How'd you like to light on a chest full of gold and silver coins—hey?"

But it roused only a faint enthusiasm, which faded out. Things were falling apart, and the pirate flag was unfurled and without breeze. Joe sat poking at the sand with a stick and looking very gloomy. Finally he threw down the stick and said:

"Oh, boys. Let's just give it up. I want to go home. It's so lonesome here."

"Oh no, Joe, you'll feel better by and by," said Tom. "Just think of the great fishing we've got here."

"I don't care for fishing anymore. I want to go home."

"Oh, shucks! You baby! You want to go home to your mother, I reckon!"

"Yes, I do," Joe said, snuffling a little. "And I ain't any more baby than you are, Mr. Smartypants."

"Fine! We'll let the baby go back home, won't we, Huck. You like it here, don't you, Huck? Well, *don't you*?"

"Ah, I like it fine," Huck said without any heart in it.

"I'll never speak to either of you again as long as I live," said Joe, standing up and kicking the stick with his foot. And he moved away from the two and began to dress himself.

"Who cares?" said Tom. "Go 'long home and get laughed at. Huck and me ain't crybabies. We'll stay, won't we, Huck? Let him go home if he wants to."

But Tom was uneasy, and was alarmed to see Joe go forward with his dressing. Without a parting word, Joe gathered up a few belongings and began to wade off toward the opposite shore. Tom glanced at Huck, who could not bear his look, and so he dropped his eyes.

"I want to go too, Tom," Huck said quietly. "It's getting lonesome here anyway, and now without Joe, it'll be worse. Let's just go."

"I won't! You can go if you want to, but I mean to stay!"

"I'm goin', then."

"Well, go then—who's stopping you?"

"Tom, I wish you'd come too. Think it over for a second. We'll wait for you when we reach the shore."

"Well, you'll be waitin' a long time, I can tell you that!"

Tom stood and watched the two of them trudge away, with a strong desire to join them. He hoped the boys would stop, but they waded on. He made one struggle with his pride, then began to run after his comrades, yelling:

"Wait! Wait! I have something to tell you!"

They presently stopped and turned around. When he got to their position, he began unfolding the delicate origami of his secret, his plan, and they listened begrudgingly until at last they saw what he was driving at, and then they let out a war whoop of applause and said his idea was splendid, splendid, and they chided him that if he had told them this before, they would never have started away.

The boys came gaily back and went at their games with a will, chattering all the time about Tom's stupendous plan and admiring the genius of it. Tom cautioned that everything would have to be just so, and they shook their heads and said it would be no problem. After a dainty turtle egg and fish dinner, Tom told Huck he wanted to learn how to smoke, and Joe said he wouldn't mind it, either. So Huck made a few quick pipes and filled them with tobacco. They stretched out on their elbows and began to puff, with tenuous confidence. The smoke had an unpleasant taste, and they gagged a little, but Tom boasted:

"Why, this is so easy! If I'd'a knowed this was all it was, I'd'a learnt long ago!"

"Me, too," said Joe, his mouth full of smoke. "It's just nothing!"

"Nothing 'tall," Tom agreed.

"Nope. Nothing," Joe said.

"I could smoke this pipe all day. But I'll tell you one thing—I bet you Jeff Hatcher couldn't."

"Nah. He'd keel right over with his first one or two draws. Just let him try it!"

"And Johnny Miller—I wish I could see Johnny Miller tackle this!"

"Oh, don't I!" said Joe. "One little puff and he'd be on the ground."

" 'Deed he would. Say—I wish the other boys could see us now."

"Jings! That'd be gay, Tom. 'Course they'd think we was Zum and they'd run for their lives!"

So the posturing went on. Presently the talk began to flag a little and grow disjointed. The silences widened, and Tom and Joe began to hang their heads like plow horses in the noonday sun. They went down to the edge of the water and doused their faces, but they both began to look pale and miserable. The pale color soon receded and left them both a pearly green. Joe said feebly:

"I think I've lost my knife. I reckon I should go fetch it."

With dry and quavering lips, Tom said:

"I'll help you, Joe. I may have lost mine too. You needn't come, Huck. We can find it." And off they staggered, into the forest.

Huck sat down and waited an hour for his friends. The sun sank into the trees and Huck started a fire for dinner. Then he began to feel lonesome, and went to find the other two. They were both apart in the woods, both very pale, both fast asleep. Something told him if they had had any trouble, they had got rid of it.

They were not talkative at dinner that night. Finally, Huck said:

"Someone tell a ghost story."

Joe began to tell a story he had heard the summer before from his uncle who was down from Ohio. It was the story of a boy who was accidentally killed by his pals and thrown into a deep quarry with chains wrapped around his arms and legs—but Joe's heart was not in it. The other boys knew the story—everyone knew the story—and Joe skipped through it, telling it too fast, touching on only a few of the high points, and by rushing the story as he did, he ruined it.

But they commended him on his effort and then Huck asked Tom if he had anything. Tom started to tell a story about their village being overrun by the dead, which was a good beginning, but he stopped and was almost embarrassed to continue. He began talking about Zum animals, undead foxes and squirrels and bats, and it wasn't really a story at all, but an unpleasant picture that had no punch line. They could see he was trying to go somewhere with it, but was holding back. The aftereffects of the tobacco had gotten to him, too, and finally he just stopped, inwardly fatigued. The crickets and the sound of the moving water were in his ears, and they all fell silent in the darkness, and soon were asleep.

About midnight, Joe awoke and called to the other boys. There was an oppressiveness in the air that seemed to bode something. The boys huddled together and fed the dying fire, quiet and waiting. The crickets had fallen silent, and the river seemed to be moving faster. All other sounds were swallowed up in the enveloping darkness. Then a faint moan came through the branches of the forest, and the boys shuddered with the idea that the spirit of the night was amongst them. There was a pause. Now a weird flash turned night into day and showed every little blade of grass, separate and distinct. A deep peal of thunder rumbled through the leaves and lost itself in the distance. The thunder was so deep and rich that the boys could feel it through the ground. All the leaves began to stir, and the campfire threw a thousand sparking embers into the trees. Another fierce glare lit up the forest and an instant later, a crash followed that seemed to explode right over the boys' heads. They clung together in terror, and a few large raindrops began falling in the trees.

"Quick, boys! Go to the tent!" exclaimed Tom.

A blast roared through the trees, making everything sing as it went. One blinding flash came after another, and there was peal after peal of deafening thunder. And now a drenching rain came down, hammering itself in sheets upon the ground. The tempest rose higher and higher, the old tent flapped furiously, until it tore loose from its moorings and went sailing up into the sky. Now the battle was at its highest. Every little while some giant tree yielded the fight and crashed with a roar through the younger growth, and the unflagging thunder came in ear-splitting, explosive bursts. It seemed to be tearing the little island to pieces, and it went on and on.

Afterwards, everything in the camp was drenched, and ruined. Presently, they discovered that their bonfire had eaten under the large, fallen log it had been built against, and there were still a few red embers ready to coax a fire back to life again.

They all concentrated on feeding the flame, and the fire began to burn anew. They piled on dead broken branches until they had a raging furnace, and were glad-hearted once more. They collected the remnants of their remaining food and had a feast, and after that sat by the fire and talked about their glorious midnight adventure until the following morning.

As the sun began to steal in upon the boys, drowsiness came over them and they went out into the sunshine to lie down and nap. They got scorched by and by, and they set about putting together a breakfast. Tom noticed the signs of homesickness begin to intrude upon their activities, and he reminded them of their glorious upcoming plan—their secret—and so sparked a note of cheer. Their play that day was subdued, and for them, peaceful.

After supper, they tried smoking again, and they found they could do so without having to go hunt for a lost knife. Now, they practiced cautiously, with right fair success, and so they spent a triumphant, if lonely evening. That night, when they turned toward sleep, Tom feared that he would dream of his village in ruin, ashes fouling the air, and a terrible black dog and its owner, but his dreams were nothing but blackness and a blanket of silence, the kind of comfortable death that had been familiar to him before everything had gone wrong.

17

The Death of Pirates

The Saturday afternoon after the storm was a solemn and forlorn time in the village. The Harpers adorned their front door with black crepe and kept themselves inside their house to grieve privately. Aunt Polly's own family was awash in tears, and though she tried to keep up with her day-to-day rituals and so be an anchor for the rest of them, she was lost in a deep sadness, and her washing went undone and the meals were not cooked. Sid and Mary stayed in their rooms, and were not mindful of things like chores and hunger. An unusual quiet possessed the entire village, and the villagers conducted their business but talked little. Even the few who were vague on the boys' identities were aware of the tragedy. The Saturday holiday seemed a burden to the children. They had no stomach for games and sports, and gave them up.

In the afternoon, Becky Thatcher found herself moping about the deserted schoolyard, feeling very melancholy. Tom was gone—her only real friend. Her parents were sympathetic and solicitous, but couldn't possibly understand how she felt. She was living with strangers, really, and she had no safe harbor to moor herself. She remembered the incident with the wildflower and Tom retrieving it, and it felt like the whole thing had happened a thousand years before. She realized she had nothing of Tom to remember him by, and she choked back a little sob. She remembered each time he tried to gain her attention, each picture he drew for her on his slate, and she thought: he's gone now. I will never, never, ever see him again.

The thought broke her down and she wandered off with tears rolling down her cheeks. Then a group of boys and girls—playmates of Tom and Joe's—came by, and stood in front of Aunt Polly's house and spoke in reverent tones of how Tom did so-and-so, the last time they saw him, and how Joe said some small thing—and each speaker pointed out the exact spot where they stood and where Joe and Tom stood—and where Huck would have stood had he come to school more often.

There was some dispute about who saw the dead boys last in life, and many claimed this dubious distinction. When it was fully decided who did see the departed last, the lucky parties took on a mantle of sacred importance and were gaped at and envied by one and all. One poor lad, who had no other grandeur to offer, said with pride that Tom had licked him once, but that bid for glory was a failure. Most of the boys could claim that distinction, but did not because of the overabundance of that commodity.

When the Sunday-school hour was finished the next morning, the church bell began to toll instead of ringing in the usual way. The villagers began to gather, loitering in the vestibule to whisper in hushed tones about the tragedy. But there was no whispering in the church itself; there was only the formal rustling of dresses as the women gathered to their seats. None could remember when the church had been so full before. There was finally a waiting pause, and Aunt Polly entered, followed closely by Sid and Mary, and then the Harper family, all in black. The whole congregation rose and stood until the mourners were seated in the front rows. There was another respectful silence, broken here and there by sobs, and then the minister clasped his hands together and prayed aloud. A hymn was sung, and the sermon that followed was based on the Biblical lesson "I am the resurrection and the life."

As the sermon proceeded, the minister drew marvelous pictures of the boys, their graces, their winning ways, and the promise of the lost boys, and every member of the congregation realized their sweet, generous nature and how awfully they would be missed. The crowd became more and more moved, until at last the whole assembly broke down and joined the mourners in anguished sobs, the preacher himself giving way to his feelings and crying in the pulpit.

There was a rustling in the small gallery over the congregation, which no one noticed; a moment later, one of the interior church doors creaked open, and the preacher's face took on a strange countenance. He raised his hands as if to guard his face, and he shrieked horribly.

First one, then all pairs of eyes followed the minister's. The three dead boys came marching up the aisle, Tom in the lead, Joe next, then Huck. Tom was still hobbling due to his inflamed toe, and all three were a ruin of drooping rags, their hair wild, their faces streaked and filthy. Had they tried to ape the gait and mannerisms of the Zum, they could not have done a better job.

Several members of the congregation cried out, a few of the older women passed out and were caught and lowered to the pews, and some of the men cried out for help, and the armed guards outside the building burst in, expecting to see something terrible and grim. When they saw the dead boys standing in front of the assembly, they cocked their weapons and moved forward looking for a clean, unobstructed shot. Aunt Polly saw the boys and automatically reached for her axe handle, which had been holstered in the vestibule. Nevertheless, the unexpectedness of the situation gave the boys a few seconds, and so they saved themselves. Joe Harper went to his mother and started sobbing as a nice defensive resource, and his mother instinctively grabbed him and began covering his pink and un-maggoty face with kisses, knowing immediately that this was the boy who had disappeared a few days before, not some undead caricature who had stumbled in to compound their misery.

Tom went to Aunt Polly, and Mary, and even Sid, and it

was immediately clear to his aunt that it was her Tom before her, silly and hugging her and wet with tears, babbling utter nonsense.

The men, slightly confused, kept their weapons raised, but uncocked their pieces. They were just boys in front of them, not Zum, it was obvious.

Aunt Polly, Mary, and the Harpers threw themselves on their loved ones, smothering them with kisses and giving prayers of thanksgiving, while poor Huck stood abashed and aloof, not knowing exactly what to do or where to hide from so many uncomfortable eyes. He wavered and began to move back, and several of the armed men were thinking of a shot, when Tom grabbed his aunt and cried:

"Oh, Aunt Polly, it ain't fair! Someone's got to be glad to see Huck, too!"

Polly was in such a joyous frenzy that she grabbed both Tom and Huck and clasped them to her bosom, crying copiously, and spoiling the shot for any of the nearby marksmen.

Suddenly the minister shouted at the top of his voice:

"Praise God from whom all blessings flow—sing!—and put your hearts into it. Gentlemen. No gunfire, please!"

And everyone did as they were asked. The whole congregation sang, shaking the rafters of the building, and it was so stirring that the marksmen rested their guns on the ground, took up hymnals, and sang along.

Tom Sawyer looked about him at the adoring adults and envious children and admitted in his heart that he had never been so happy in his life. The hymnal was the end of the service, and it then fell apart in a sea of chaos, hugs and kisses and happy embraces. After a time, the armed guards heard the report of distant shots from another village, and withdrew to offer their assistance. It was an intrusion by two Zum, and by the time they arrived, they had both been dispatched. The guards made a grim inspection of the undead souls, but neither was anyone they had ever seen before, no one from their village, and they headed back to town to see what else they had missed in the moments since they were gone.

18

A Glorious Aftermath

That was Tom's great plan and great secret—the scheme to return home with his brother pirates and attend their own funerals. He had thought of every detail, only missing the nervous consternation that would come from the armed guards that had very nearly resulted in the need for a second wave of mourning and funerals. The boys had paddled over to the Missouri shore on a log, at dusk on Saturday, landing five or six miles below the village; they slept that night in the woods at the edge of town till almost daylight, then crept through the back alleys and lanes, finishing their sleep in the as yet unguarded church, among the hard wooden benches in the gallery.

At breakfast on Monday, Tom's family was very loving, and very attentive to his wants. There was an unusual amount of talk. Polly's joy and relief had bubbled over into endless, happy chatter. In the course of it, she said:

"Well, it was a fine joke, Tom, to keep everyone sufferin' all week long so you boys had a good time, but it is a pity you could be so hard-hearted as to let me suffer so. You could have come over and given me a hint some way that you warn't dead, but only run off."

"Yes, you could have," said Mary; "and I believe you would have if you had thought of it."

Tom could not think of the right answer. "I—well, I don't know. 'T'would have spoiled everything."

"Tom, I hoped you loved me that much," said Aunt Polly, with a grieved tone that discomforted the boy.

"Now Auntie," Mary jumped in; "it's only Tom's giddy way—you know how he is—he never thinks of anything."

Aunt Polly shook her head. "Sid would have thought of it. Tom, you'll look back some day, when it's too late, and you'll wish you'd cared a little more for me when it would cost you so little."

"Now, Auntie, I do care for you." He had an inspiration. "But I dreamed about you, anyway. That's something, ain't it?"

"It ain't much, but it's better than nothin'. What did you dream?"

"Why, I dreamt you was sitting over there by the bed, and Sid was sitting by the woodbox, and Mary was next to him. And I dreamt that Joe Harper's mother was here too."

"Why, she *was* here. Was that all there was to it?"

"Oh, there was lots more. Somehow it seems to me that the wind—the wind blowed the candle—"

"Mercy! Go on, Tom—go on!"

"And you believed the door was open, and you made Sid go and shut it."

Aunt Polly was clutching her throat with her hands. "Well, land's sake! Don't tell me there ain't nothing in dreams. Go on, Tom."

"And then you began to cry. And Mrs. Harper did too, and said Joe was just the same way, and she wished she hadn't whipped him for taking some cream when she'd throwed it out her own self—"

"Tom! The spirit was upon you! You was a-prophesying—that's what you was doin'! Land alive, go on!"

"Then Sid said he hoped I was better off where I was gone to, but if I'd been better sometimes—and you stopped him and shut him up sharp."

"I did indeed! There must have been an angel there somewheres."

"And Mrs. Harper told you about Joe settin' off a fire-cracker under her, and you told her about me and the cat and the Painkiller."

"It happened just so! As sure as I'm a-sitting in this very chair. Tom, you couldn't told it more like if you'd a-seen it! Then what? Go on."

"Then you went to bed, and I wrote on a piece of sycamore bark *'We ain't dead—we are only off being pirates,'* and put it on the table by the candle; and then I went over and kissed you on the cheek."

"Did you, Tom, did you? I just forgive you everything for that!" And she seized the boy in a crushing hug that made him feel like the guiltiest of villains. But Tom had a head of steam, and continued.

"There was still more, Auntie. But it gets kind of bad."

"I don't care, Tom. This is some kind of gift you have. Go on and tell me the whole thing."

"I went back into the village, but it was all empty. There was nobody left I could see. I could hear cryin' and sobbin' and people in pain, but couldn't find a soul. I couldn't find you."

Aunt Polly simply patted him on the head.

"There was smoke and ash in the air, and the houses were all empty, or deserted, or in flame. It was the end of things."

"Mercy!" Polly exclaimed.

"And I went to our front door, but it had been splintered in and ripped off the hinges. I ran upstairs and hid myself under the covers."

"Land sakes, this is an evil dream, Tom. Mercy! Go on! Let's hear it all."

Tom could not tell her the rest of it. He had hurt her enough. The first part of the dream was all marvels and delight, but his real dream, the one that came back to him night after night, was nothing like this. He could not tell her about the black dog that prowled his dreams, its long, gray teeth poking through the holes in its cheek as if it had been devouring itself, the clumps of fur sloughing off as it walked, the fat maggots writhing and glistening as they fell onto the cold ground. And he could not tell her about Injun

Joe, because it frightened him even to think about it, and it would frighten his aunt, too.

"That's all there was," Tom lied.

Polly breathed a sigh of relief.

The children soon left for school, and Polly went to call on Mrs. Harper to recount Tom's marvelous dream. She too abridged the tale and ended it with Tom kissing her on the cheek. Nothing more really needed to be said.

At school, what a hero Tom had become! It was as if he had been the drummer at the head of a procession or the elephant leading a great circus into town. Boys of his own age pretended not to know he had been away at all, but they were consumed with envy, nevertheless. The school made so much of him and Joe that the two heroes were not long in becoming insufferably stuck up. Finally, when they took out their new pipes and went about serenely puffing— even though they had no tobacco—the very summit of glory had been reached.

Tom decided he would be independent of Becky Thatcher now. The glory was sufficient. Now that he was the hero he was, perhaps she would be wanting to make up with him. Well, let her—she would see that he could be as indifferent as some other people he could name. Presently she arrived, and Tom pretended not to see her. He moved away and joined a group of boys and girls and began to talk. Soon he noticed that she too was avoiding him, pretending to be busy chasing schoolmates, and capturing them always in his vicinity. It gratified his vanity, and made him even more resolute to avoid her. Presently she gave up her skylarking, and sat close to him, sighing once or twice, ignoring him and every-one else, and occasionally glancing wistfully at him. Tom was talking to Amy Lawrence more than anyone else. Becky felt a sharp pang and grew disturbed and uneasy—jealous. She tried to move away, but her feet betrayed her and carried her into the group instead. She began speaking with a sham vivacity, inviting all the boys and girls to a special picnic her parents were permitting her. They were concerned with their daughter's constant sadness, and thought up the idea to bring her more comrades and friends.

She invited everyone who seemed to be interested—everyone but Tom, who continued to talk to Amy about his adventures and the terrible storm on the island.

"You going to have all the girls and boys?" one of the less popular girls wondered.

"Yes, yes, everyone!"

"Oh, may I come?" said Gracie Miller.

"Yes."

"And me?" said Sally Rogers.

"Yes."

"And me, too?" said Susy Harper. "And Joe?"

"Yes, yes, of course."

Wouldn't her concerned parents be surprised that she had invited the entire class—everyone but Tom and Amy. Tom turned coolly away, still talking, and took Amy with him. Becky's legs trembled and tears came into her eyes; she hid these signs and went on chattering, but the thrill had gone out of the picnic now, and out of everything else. She went away from the group as soon as she could and had a good cry. There she sat, till the bell rang, and she roused herself up, with a vindictive cast in her eye, and she thought: she knew what *she'd* do.

At recess, Tom continued his flirtation with Amy with great self-satisfaction. He found Becky, who was sitting cozily on a little bench behind the schoolhouse looking at a book with Alfred Temple. They were so absorbed that they did not seem to be conscious of anything else in the world. Jealousy ran hot through Tom's veins, and he began to hate himself for throwing away the one chance Becky had given him for a reconciliation. He left them there, but drifted back again and again to sear his eyeballs on the hateful spectacle. He called himself a fool and began to feel miserable again.

Amy's prattle became intolerable, and Tom hinted at important things he had to attend to. The girl seemed oblivious to this, and chirped on. At last, he said he *had* to go about attending to these things—and she said she would be around for him after school.

Tom fled home from school at noon. He could endure no more of it. Becky resumed her picture inspections with Alfred, but as Tom was no longer there, her concentration waned and she lost interest. Two or three times she pricked up her ears at approaching footsteps, but it was a false hope. No Tom came. Soon she was utterly miserable and wished she hadn't carried her ruse so far. Poor Alfred could see he was losing her, but could not understand how. She then lost patience and said, "Oh, stop bothering me! I don't care for any pictures!" and burst into tears.

Alfred tried to comfort her, but she stopped and said:

"Go away and leave me alone, can't you! I hate you!"

Alfred went and sat alone in back of the deserted schoolhouse. He was humiliated and angry. He easily figured out the truth—that he had been a convenient prop for her to vent her spite on Tom Sawyer. He wished there was some way to get that boy into trouble without much risk to himself. Tom's spelling book fell under his eye. Here was his opportunity. He opened to the lesson for that afternoon and poured ink upon the page.

Becky, glancing in at a window, discovered Alfred in the act, and resolved to find Tom and tell him. He would be thankful, and their troubles would be healed. Soon, however, she changed her mind. She was determined to see him whipped on account of the damaged book's condition, and intended to hate him forever in the bargain.

19

Tom Tells the Truth

Tom arrived home in a dreary mood, and the first thing his aunt said to him brought his sorrows to a new and deeper level.

"Tom, I've a notion to skin you alive!"

"Auntie, what have I done?"

"You've done enough. Here I go over to the Harpers' like an old softy, expecting I'm going to make her believe all that rubbish about your dream, when lo and behold she's found out from Joe that you were over here that night, hidin' under that very table. Tom, I don't know what will become of a boy who acts like that. It makes me feel bad that you would let me make such a fool of myself and not even say a word."

It had seemed like such a good joke before—ingenious— and now it seemed mostly mean and shabby. Tom hung his head and could not think of anything to say. Eventually he said:

"Auntie, I knew it was mean, but I didn't mean it to be. I didn't. Honest! And besides, I didn't come over here to laugh at you that night."

"Then why did you come, Tom?"

"It was to tell you not to worry about us, because we hadn't gotten drownded."

"Tom. Tom, I would be the thankfullest soul in the whole world if I could believe you ever had as good a thought as that, but you know you never did—and I know it, Tom."

"Indeed I did, Auntie. I did! May I roam the world as a Zum if I'm lyin'!"

"Don't talk that way, Tom. Don't do it. It only makes a bad thing a hundred times worse."

"It ain't a lie, Auntie. It's the truth. I wanted to keep you from grieving—that's the only reason I came back."

"I'd give the world to believe that—it would cover up everything else. But it ain't reasonable, Tom—because in the end, you *didn't* tell me."

"Well, see, when you got to talkin' about the funeral, I just got all fun of the idea of the three of us comin' back and hidin' in the church, and I couldn't bear to spoil it. So I just put the sycamore bark back in my pocket and kept mum."

"What sycamore bark?"

"The bark I wrote on to tell you what we were doin'. I wish now you'd woke up when I kissed you on the cheek and said good-bye."

The hard lines on his aunt's face relaxed and a sudden tenderness dawned in her eyes.

"You kissed me on the cheek, Tom?"

"Why, yes. I did."

"And why was that?"

"Because I loved you so, and you were layin' there all moanin', and I was sorry."

The words sounded like the truth. The old lady could not hide a tremor in her voice when she said: "We'll never know, then, will we? You and your stories. Be off to school, now, and don't bother me no more."

The moment he was out the door, she went to the closet to retrieve the ruin of a jacket Tom had gone pirating in. A moment later, she was reading Tom's piece of bark through flowing tears, and saying: "I could forgive this boy if he'd committed a million sins." She took the sycamore bark note and put it in a small jewelry box with some earrings and brooches, and other of her small treasures. Then she lay her axe handle next to the bed, pulled a rumpled handkerchief out of her bosom, and wiped away a lingering tear.

20

Becky's Dilemma

There was something about Aunt Polly's manner that swept away Tom's low spirits and made him lightheaded and happy again. He started to school and had the luck of coming upon Becky Thatcher at the head of Meadow Lane. His mood always determined his manner, and without a moment of hesitation he ran up to her and said:

"I acted mighty mean today, Becky, and I'm so sorry. I won't ever, ever do that again as long as I live—please make up with me, won't you?"

The girl stopped and looked him scornfully in the face:

"I'll thank you to keep to yourself, Mr. Thomas Sawyer. I'm never going to speak to you again."

She tossed her head and went on. Tom was so stunned that he had not even the presence of mind to say "Who cares, Miss Smartypants?" until the moment was over and it was too late. So he said nothing. He was in a fine rage, nevertheless. He presently encountered her again in the schoolyard and delivered a stinging remark as he passed. She hurled one in return, and the breach was complete. So hot was her resentment that she could not wait for school to begin to see Tom flogged for his ink-stained spelling book. If she had any lingering notion of exposing Alfred Temple, Tom's offensive tone had driven it out of her mind completely.

Poor thing, she did not know how fast she was approaching trouble herself. The schoolmaster, Mr. Dobbins, had reached middle age with an unsatisfied ambition. He wanted nothing more than to be a military man, a leader of other men, specifically a cavalryman, some sort of national hero, but fate had decreed that he be nothing more than a village schoolteacher. Every day he took a mysterious book out of his desk and absorbed himself in it when no children were reciting. He kept that book under lock and key. Every boy and girl had a theory on the nature of this book, but no two theories were alike, and there was no good way of getting at the facts in the case. Now, as Becky was passing the desk, she noticed that the key was in the lock! It was a precious moment. She glanced around and found herself alone, and the next moment the book was in her hands. The title page gave her a hint as to its contents: *The Awful Disclosures of Maria Monk.* Curious, she began to turn the pages. Almost immediately, she came on a number of black-and-white drawings—women bound in leather straps, others being branded with hot irons. Another drawing showed a man in religious garb throwing a tiny baby in a dark and horrible pit with obvious relish. A third showed a number of men and women in religious apparel praying over a Zum who had been tied and bound to a large wooden stake. At that moment, a shadow fell on the page, startling her, and Tom Sawyer caught a brief glimpse of the picture. Becky snatched at the book to close it, and had the bad luck to tear the pictured plate half down the middle. She thrust the volume back into the desk, turned the key, and burst out crying in shame and vexation.

"Tom Sawyer, you are just as mean as you can be, sneaking up on a person just to see what they're looking at."

"How could I know you were looking at anything?"

"You ought to be ashamed of yourself, Tom Sawyer. You know you're going to tell on me, and oh, what shall I do, what shall I do! I'll be whipped, and I was never whipped at school before, neither here nor overseas."

She stamped her little foot in frustration and said:

"Be mean if you want to. I know something that's going to happen. You just wait and see if you want! Hateful, hateful, hateful!" and she left the schoolhouse with a new explosion of crying.

Tom stood still, rather flustered by her behavior. Presently he said to himself:

"What a curious kind of fool girls are. Never been licked in school before! Shucks. What's so big about it? That's just like a girl—thin-skinned and chicken-hearted. Well, I ain't goin' to tell Old Dobbins on Becky because there's other ways of gettin' even that ain't so mean. Old Dobbins will figure it all out by himself. He'll just ask everybody who tore the book—first one, then t'other, and when he comes to the right girl, he'll know it without anyone sayin' a word. Girls' faces always tell on them. And then she'll get a lickin', and there ain't no way for her out of it."

Tom joined the mob of scholars outside the schoolhouse for a few moments, and the master arrived and took them in. Every time Tom glanced at the girls' side of the room, Becky's face troubled him. Considering everything, he did not want to pity her, and yet he did. Presently, the matter of Tom's ruined spelling book was discovered; Becky surmised that Tom could not get out of his trouble by denying his involvement, and she was right. The denial only seemed to infuriate the master further.

Tom took his whipping and went back to his seat not at all broken-hearted, for he thought it entirely possible that he unknowingly upset the ink on the spelling book himself. He denied it initially for form's sake and because that was his usual custom, and stuck to the denial on general principles.

A whole hour drifted by, the master nodding on his throne, the air drowsy with the hum of study. By and by, Mr. Dobbins straightened himself up, yawned, then unlocked his desk and reached for his book. He fingered the book absently for a while, then took it out and settled himself in his chair to read. Tom shot a glance at Becky. He had seen a hunted and helpless rabbit look as she did, with a gun leveled at its head. Instantly, he forgot his quarrel with her. Something had to be done, and quickly. But the imminence of the emergency paralyzed his invention. The master opened the book and it was too late. There was no help for Becky now. The next moment, the master discovered the tear and he stood and faced the school. Even the innocent were struck by the intensity of his gaze. There was silence while one might count to ten—the master was gathering his wrath. Then he spoke:

"Who tore this book?"

There was not a sound. One could have heard a pin drop. The stillness continued, and the master searched face after face for signs of guilt.

"Benjamin Rogers, did you tear this book?"

A denial. Another pause.

"Joseph Harper, did you?"

Another denial. Tom's uneasiness grew more and more intense under the slow torture of the proceedings. Then the master turned to the girls:

"Amy Lawrence?"

A shake of the head.

"Gracie Miller?"

The same sign.

"Susan Harper, did you do this?"

Another negative. The next girl was Becky Thatcher. Tom was trembling from head to toe with the hopelessness of the situation.

"Rebecca Thatcher?"

Tom glanced at her face—it was pale in terror, and her hands rose to her mouth in fear, shame, and misery.

"Did you tear this book?"

A thought sprang like lightning through Tom's brain. He sprang to his feet and shouted, "I done it!"

The school stared in puzzlement at this incredible and unexpected folly. Tom stepped forward to receive his punishment, ready to absorb the most merciless flogging that Mr. Dobbins had ever administered. Becky's eyes were shiny, and Tom realized this would be his second whipping of the day. But just as Mr. Dobbins raised his cane, a shot rang out from just outside the schoolroom door, a brief, startled cry from the guard and a brief, intense struggle was heard, and the door swung open, bringing in the smell of rotting meat, decaying flesh, and death.

21

The Battle at the Schoolhouse

The children screamed in panic, knocking over their desks and each other in the effort to work their way to the back of the room. It was not an orderly retreat, and some of the children leapt over each other, knocking others to the ground. The boys and girls pitched themselves out of the open windows, some helping each other, others just throwing themselves out any way they could, hitting the ground, gathering themselves up, and sprinting as fast as they could to put some distance between themselves and the schoolhouse. The children who could not immediately gain access to the windows pushed themselves against the back wall, cowering, backing into each other, pinning the smallest boys and girls against the wall until they were helpless and unable to move.

The Zum had come upon old Mr. Branson asleep, and by

the time the guard awoke, it was too late. The Zum was upon him, tearing the poor man with his hands and teeth. The one shot that was fired went harmlessly through the Zum's rib cage, and so did nothing to slow the advance. Mr. Branson broke free and retreated a few feet into the school yard to collect himself and try to load his gun for another shot. He cursed himself for dozing in the afternoon sun, but immediately put it behind him. The sounds of terror in the schoolhouse roused him to action, and he grabbed a leg of the ruined chair he had been sleeping in and came in after his attacker.

The Zum had been a large man, and probably muscular. He had had shoulder-length hair and the clothes of one who does strenuous work for a living—a blacksmith, perhaps, or a farmer. He had been dead a long time, and his clothes, and skin, were tattered and in ribbons. There were maggots at work on his hands and his back and in his hair, and the smell was overwhelming.

Tom had frozen for a second, waiting for his whipping to commence. Moments after the door was thrown open, he looked around for Mr. Dobbins, and realized he was no longer present in the schoolroom. He had been one of the first out of the window. It came to the schoolmaster that his selfish actions would mean the termination of his employment, but he didn't care, not then, nor the day after, nor the day after that. In fact, the schoolmaster seemed to vanish from the face of the earth after that morning, and everyone had a good idea why—he had abandoned a classroom full of defenseless children, the village's children, and though everyone understood his motivation, no one could bring themselves to sympathize. Had he shown up demanding a final paycheck, it might have crystallized the villagers' attitude a little more concerning his actions, and it might have accounted for the second biggest surprise in his life.

Tom observed the chaos for a second or two and watched the children pour out of the windows. Becky had not been in the first wave of survivors, and stood shrieking and crying within the group of children huddled together against the back of the room. Tom saw Joe Harper out of the corner of his eye and turned. Joe had grabbed the classroom flagpole and was attempting to crack the Zum over the head with it. In other circumstances it might have been funny, Joe waving the flag madly back and forth in the little room, as if he was trying to get someone's attention, or was being bad and showing off. The Zum fended off Joe's attack but didn't seem to be able to grab the pole out of his hands. A lot of the meat was gone from the Zum's hands, and most of the fingers had fallen off.

Tom looked around for something he could use to help assist his friend, but he could find no weapons. He pulled out the knife Mary had given him and knew it was not enough for the battle. While Joe harried the Zum with the flagpole, Tom ran to the abandoned schoolmaster's desk and looked there. There was a nice-sized stone bust of George Washington, and without thinking, he picked it up and threw it at the Zum's head. It glanced off its chest and fell to the ground. So much for that idea.

The retired Mr. Branson came in through the door and

told everyone to flee, flee for their lives! And that was what most of the children were in the process of doing. The boys and girls at the back of the classroom were no longer considering the windows, and seemed frozen, unable to move. Something had happened to them, and they were rooted to the spot, clinging to each other helplessly, gripped by fear or some other nameless and even more terrifying emotion. The guard grabbed the Zum from behind, and the monster let out a terrific low moan and began thrashing back and forth, like a large animal of the forest trying to shake a wolf off its back. Tom picked up the bust of Washington and threw it again, and this time he missed his mark completely, and the bust went rolling out the front door and into the abandoned school yard.

Joe Harper went at the Zum again and again, and Tom realized the creature was not using its arms to protect its head. Unlike Joe, however, the Zum was not tiring. It cried out in rage and began moving forward, and Joe began moving backward, threading his way carefully around the fallen and overturned desks, desperate not to fall over, or he would be lost forever. Though he had been to his funeral once and found it delightful, Tom had no wish to go again. But the attack was taking a toll on Joe's energies, and he began to pant, his arms began to ache, there was a stitch in his side from the panting. He looked around quickly to see what other options he had, and found none.

In similar desperation, Tom picked up one of the slates that had been strewn around the floor and pulled off the wooden trim, exposing the uneven, ragged edges. An idea struck him. He had once skipped a stone fourteen times in a contest with Joe, Huck, and some of the other boys. On flat water, the record was forty-two skips. Using the same technique, he took the slate and threw it at the advancing Zum, who seemed to be concentrating on Joe. It caught the guard on the wrist, and he pulled his arm back, wincing in considerable pain.

Tom picked up another slate and took the opportunity to throw it, and then another. His aim improved with each throw. Each one was hitting the Zum in the chest and face, some with more effect than others. On the fifth throw, the slate caught the Zum cleanly in the throat, and tissue and muscle were severed. The head leaned to one side and would not right itself.

"Keep whackin' him, Joe!" Tom screamed.

Joe did not have the energy to respond, but knew what he was supposed to do. He jabbed the Zum again and again, on one side of the head, then the other, trying to knock it loose. The Zum flailed its arms and knocked the pole completely out of Joe's hands, and Tom took the opportunity to throw his best shot. The slate hit the same neck area and stuck, embedded in the tissues.

The Zum advanced on Joe Harper, who had crumpled to the ground and was gasping in exhaustion. It stood over the boy in triumph and began lowering itself as if to feed, reaching for him, a thick, pink, ropy slime oozing out of its skull and what was left of its mouth. Maggots and insects dislodged by the flagpole rained out of the Zum's hair and beard onto Joe's face. Tom ran forward. He had run out of ideas, but couldn't bear to see his comrade torn apart, an event that seemed only seconds away. Raising his final slate, he hurled it at the Zum from just a foot or two away, and it drove itself into the already embedded slate, exploding in a rain of rock fragments. The Zum's head slumped completely sideways, hanging on with just a few ragged bits of skin and muscle. Tom grabbed Joe's flagpole just as the Zum lowered itself to feast on the small boy, and whirled it through the air, striking the head like a well-hit baseball in a summer's game. The head completely disconnected from the body and rolled out the front door, landing several feet from the bust of George Washington. The rest of the thing wavered for a moment and came crashing down on the schoolhouse floor next to Joe like a pile of garbage.

"Tom!" Joe gasped. He was pale and shaken, almost surprised to still be alive. "You kilt it!"

Tom was not yet thinking about what this would mean as far as his currency in the village. He had come to his own funeral, and would bask in that glory for an entire summer. This, however, was something else. He could not get his head around what this was going to do to his reputation. He knew it was a good thing, though—defending the school, saving his best friend's life, and destroying a much larger foe, all of it in front of a girl whose attention he had been desperately seeking. His head could not accept any more, at least for the present.

"We certainly did, Joe. We certainly did!"

By the time Tom went to bed that night—and it was well past his normal bedtime, as a parade of friends and neighbors wanted to hear the story again and again—he felt a changed person in ways he could not explain. He had broken Mr. Branson's wrist, and the man sobbed and thanked him and could not hug him enough. Tom apologized for the accident, and Mr. Branson kissed him on the cheek and said he was not to say another word about it. Then he asked Tom to forgive *him* for falling asleep that morning and allowing the whole horrible thing to take place. "Sure," Tom responded, and the poor man began crying again, calling Tom a saint and a real asset to the whole community.

Joe Harper and Tom didn't speak to each other much after the attack, mostly because almost immediately, people began to pour into the schoolhouse with guns and pitchforks and axe handles, and the children were one by one whisked away by their loving parents to be hugged and doted over for their part in the saga. Becky came up to Tom briefly and threw her arms around him, and it had nothing to do with saving her from a caning. "Tom," she whispered into his ear emotionally, "how *could* you be so noble!"

When he fell asleep at last that night, Becky's words hung dreamily in his ear. Aunt Polly settled into a chair next to his bed with a cup of strong tea, her axe handle next to the chair. She had no idea what she was doing, but she felt very protective of her boy, and wanted to be near if he awoke with bad dreams or a case of the fantods.

In the following week, the school had a small graduation. The schoolroom was scrubbed from top to bottom, vases of flowers were set on the vacant schoolmaster's desk, and a few of the retired schoolmarms hammered together a program that featured recitations, geography and spelling awards, and enough pomp to please any of the parents in attendance. At the culmination of the ceremony, before everyone went outside for lemonade and a variety of trifles, the mayor of the village delivered a special award—one to Joe Harper and one to Tom Sawyer. He made a warm speech on how they were the two most shiningest examples of citizens on the planet, and that the whole town was proud of them, and beholden to them for their role in staving off what might have been a considerable tragedy. The boys put the medals around their necks and resolved never to take them off, even when swimming, or sleeping, or bathing. Every time Tom glanced at Becky, she was gazing at him, and she did not look away when she noticed he was looking at her. Tom took this as a very, very good sign.

22

Post-Graduation Ennui

After graduation, Tom's notoriety remained at a high level, and several adults, old Mr. Branson among them—who was on the mend nicely with his arm in a neat sling—urged him to join a new group of youth in town, called the Cadets of Temperance. They talked about it and made it seem like a once-in-a-lifetime opportunity, and as Tom had little else to occupy his time, he decided to give it a try. He was initially attracted by their special caps and uniforms, especially a lavish red sash that was worn at all formal events. He promised to abstain from smoking, drinking, and profanity as long as he remained a member. He discovered that to promise not to do a thing is the surest way in the world to make a person want to do that very thing. Tom soon found himself tormented with a constant desire to drink and smoke, and nothing but the prospect of walking around in an uncomfortable

woolen uniform with a bright silk sash kept him from resigning from the organization.

The Fourth of July was coming up and the Cadets of
Temperance would be marching in the parade, but Tom
didn't think he'd have to wait that long to display his red
sash. He fixed his hopes upon old Judge Frazier, justice of
the peace, who was said to be on his deathbed and would
have a large, public funeral, since he was so high an official.
The Cadets would be marching in this funeral, either di-
rectly in front of the hearse wagon, or just in back of it.
Some of the cadets would be carrying colorful flags and
banners *besides* the wonderful silk sash. Some evenings his
hopes flew so high that he put on his regalia and practiced
marching, mournfully, up and down in front of a full-length
mirror. But the judge had a discouraging way of fluctuating.
After several days near death, he was pronounced upon the
mend—and soon after that convalescent. Tom was disgusted,
and handed in his resignation at once. That same night, the
judge took a turn for the worse, and Tom ran to the judge's
house to see what he could for himself. Just when he arrived,
a grim-faced physician came out of the house carrying a
large canvas bag, big enough for a small melon. Tom asked
how the judge was feeling, and the physician held up the bag
and just said, "He's gone." Tom realized the physician had
taken off the head as a safety measure, so as not to put a colorful postscript on an otherwise praiseworthy career in public service.

The funeral was a fine thing. The cadets paraded in a
style calculated to kill the recent member with envy. Tom

was a free boy again—that was something—but he found to his surprise that the urge to drink and smoke and swear had gone away again. The simple fact that he could do these things took most of the desire and charm away from them.

The coveted summer vacation was beginning to lay a little heavy on his hands. After the earlier excitement with the Zum invading the schoolhouse, life in the little village seemed a bit boring. He began a diary, but found nothing worth recording during the first seven days. When he did put down a brief note on his activities, he came back a few days later and was dissatisfied with the way his whole life was going.

Wednesday. Pancakes in the morning. Walked to the quarry with Huck, Joe, and others. Joe's foot swollen. Huck—infestation of some kind. Bedbugs? I tried to breathe underwater. Don't do this again!

Several similarly flat and lackluster entries made him abandon the whole experiment.

A group of performers came into town and were a sensation. They sang, and performed in a number of mildly amusing skits. Tom and Joe put together a similar troupe and kept themselves busy for two days.

Even the glorious Fourth of July was a failure, for it rained hard the entire day—and the parades and fireworks were canceled in consequence. The appearance of a U.S. senator, Mr. Busey, was an overwhelming disappointment—for he was not twenty-five feet tall as a few of the boys had promised, nor was he anywhere in the neighborhood of it. The senator made a short, impassioned speech in the town hall that evening, but Tom and most other children in the village were not inclined to go. In the middle of the senator's speech, a lone Zum was spotted in the area, and a sentry's warning shot not only brought a half-dozen marksmen to the scene, but also brought the senator to his knees, cowering behind an inadequate wooden lectern, where he stayed until hooting and catcalls from the audience brought him back to his feet. Mr. Busey apologized for the apparent timidity, but the community as a whole looked at him differently after this, and he never again won a majority of the popular vote in the surrounding area.

A circus came into town the following week, and the boys played circus for three days afterward, setting up tents, putting together acts, even charging a small admission of a few pennies to the members of the audience. The audience, who were fighting the same battle against constant summer boredom, grabbed at anything to make the hours fly.

There were a few boys-and-girls' parties, but they were so few and so fun that they only made the aching voids between them ache the harder.

Next came a bout of the measles. Tom lay a prisoner, dead to the world, for close to two weeks. No one was allowed to visit, no messages were taken, and the only person he saw regularly was Aunt Polly, who had had the measles decades earlier and was not afraid of contracting them again.

He was very ill, and interested in nothing. His dreams were fevered, disconnected, and not so much fearsome as odd and puzzling. When at last he got to his feet, a melancholy change had come over every creature. There had been a revival, spirited and popular, and everyone had gone several times just to hear how the Lord was going to smite the unbelievers. The unifying theme of the revival seemed to have something to do with faith and a contrite heart, and that a lack of faith had somehow brought the Zum out of the earth, and a renewed faith and diligence to His Word would bring an end to all of it. It was a powerful message, and universally popular. He went to call on Joe Harper, who was memorizing verses from Revelation, purely for their shock value. He sought Ben Rogers, who had begun visiting the cemetery every morning to cleanse the area with the power of prayer. He hunted up Jim Hollis, who called attention to Tom's measles and suggested sincerely that earnest prayer might have warded them off. Every boy he contacted added more weight to his depression. In desperation, he flew to Huckleberry Finn, who received Tom with scripture. His heart broke and he crept home to bed, realizing he alone of everyone in town was utterly lost. Tom, the vanquisher of Zum, was damned and going to hell. There was no other way to look at it. It wasn't fair.

The following morning, a doctor came to visit Tom again; he had relapsed. The three weeks he spent on his back this time seemed an eternity, the burning and frivolous wasting of an entire summer. When he arose at last, he found Jim Hollis acting as judge and jury in an open-air court that was trying a cat for murder, in the presence of its victim, a defenseless robin. He found Joe Harper and Huck Finn farther down a remote alleyway eating a stolen watermelon. Poor doomed lads! The whole town had fallen back into their previous sinful ways, and Tom was no longer alone.

23

Muff's Trial

At last the sleepy atmosphere of the summer was shaken—
and vigorously: Muff Potter's murder trial came in to the
court. It became the topic of village talk and gossip immediately. Tom could not get away from it. Every reference to the
murder sent a cold shudder to his heart, for his troubled conscience and fears persuaded him that the remarks were
being put to him as "feelers"; he could not imagine how he
could be suspected of knowing anything further about the
murder, but it all made him very uncomfortable. He took
Huck to a lonely place to have a talk with him. He wanted
to assure himself that Huck had remained discreet, and that
only the two of them were harboring the same awful secret.

"Huck, have you told anybody about—that?"

" 'Bout what?"

"You know what."

"Oh. Course I haven't."

"Not a word?"

"Not a one, so help me. Why d'you ask?"

"Well, I was afear'd."

"Why, Tom Sawyer, we wouldn't stay alive for two days if that got found out. You know that."

Tom felt more comfortable in the knowledge that Huck was taking the whole thing seriously. After a pause:

"Huck, no one could get you to tell, could they?"

"Get me to tell? Why, only if I wanted that murderous devil Joe to drownd me could they get me to tell. Ain't no other way."

"Well, all right, then. I guess we're safe as long as the both of us stay mum. But let's swear again anyway. It's more surer."

"Agreed."

So they swore again with grave solemnity.

"What's the talk about, Huck? It's all I seem to hear."

"Me, too. It's just Muff Potter, Muff Potter, Muff Potter all the time. It keeps me in a sweat so much I want to go off and hide till this whole thing is over."

"It's the same with me. I reckon he's a goner. Do you feel sorry for him, sometimes?"

"Most always. He ain't ever done anything to hurt anybody. Just fishes a little to get money to drink on, that's all. He loafs around considerable, but Lord, we all do that. Deep down he's a good sort. He gave me half a fish once, when they weren't enough for two, and lots of times he's kind of stood by me when I was out of luck."

"Huck, he's mended kites for me, and knitted hooks onto my line. I wish't we could get him out of there."

Huckleberry gave Tom a bemused look. "We couldn't get him out of there, Tom, and besides, 'twouldn't do him any good; they'd ketch him again and put him back in."

"Yes, I suppose. But I hate to hear them all talk about him so—leastways when he never done—you know—that."

"Lord, Tom, I hear 'em say he's the bloodiest villain in the country, and wonder why he's never been hung before."

"I hear 'em say that if he was to get set free, they'd just lynch him."

"And I believe they'd do it, too."

The boys talked long and passionately, but it brought them no comfort. As the day grew on, they did as they had done before—and went to the cell grating and gave Potter some tobacco and matches. He was on the ground floor and as usual, there were no guards posted.

His gratitude for their little kindnesses always gnawed at their conscience, and this time, it cut deeper than ever. They felt cowardly and treacherous when Potter said:

"You've been right good to me, boys, and I won't forget it. Often I say to myself, I says, 'I used to mend their kites and show them where the good fishing holes was, and now they've forgot old Muff when he's in trouble; but Tom don't, and Huck don't—they don't forget him, and I don't forget them.' Well boys, I done an awful thing—and now I got to swing for it, and it's only right. Right, and the best thing, too, I reckon. What I want to say is, don't you two ever get drunk—and you won't ever get here. It's surely a comfort to see friendly faces when you're in a muck of trouble, and there ain't none come see me but yourn. Thank you boys, thank you. I know you've helped all you can, and you'd help more if you could. Remember me."

Tom went home in misery, and his dreams that night were full of horror. When he finally went through the splintered door of his house to escape under the covers of his bed, Muff was sitting in a little chair in the corner of the room, sobbing like a baby. Tom told Muff to hide, hide! before the black dog and its owner slowly climbed the stairs and found them, but Muff just shook his head and said it was no use. He moved aside the collar of his shirt and showed Tom the burn marks from the hanging rope, and thanked Tom again for being his friend to the last. Then Muff heard something at the door, his eyes grew frightened and round, and he pointed for Tom to look—which is when Tom woke up.

The next several days, Tom hung about the courtroom, drawn by an almost irresistible impulse to go in. Huck was having the same experience. They tried to avoid each other at these times. Tom kept his ears open when people sauntered out of the courtroom, and invariably heard distressing news. Everyone's mind seemed to be made up. Injun Joe's testimony was firm and unshaken, and there was not the slightest question as to what the jury's verdict was going to be.

Tom was out late that night, and came to bed through the window. He was in a tremendous state of excitement. The entire village flocked to the courtroom the next day, for this was to be the final day of the trial, the grand day. The spectator area in back of the courtroom was packed, men and women equally. The jury came in and took their places; shortly afterward, Potter, pale and haggard, tired and hopeless, was brought in, chains on his arms and legs. No less conspicuous was Injun Joe, stolid and repellent as ever.

There was another pause, and the judge entered in his robes, and the sheriff proclaimed that court was now in session. The first witness was called, who testified that he found Muff Potter washing in the brook, early in the morning shortly after the murder, and that he immediately sneaked away. After a few more questions, the prosecutor said in a loud, clear voice:

"Take the witness."

Muff's counsel rose and said:

"I have no questions for him."

The next witness explained the finding of a knife next to the corpse, and several questions were asked. Then the prosecuting attorney said:

"Take the witness."

"I have no questions to ask him," Potter's lawyer replied.

Several more witnesses came and went, and counsel for Muff Potter declined to question any of them. The crowd in the courtroom began to murmur in annoyance. Did the attorney intend to throw away his client's life without putting forth the least effort? Several more witnesses came to the stand, but none of them were cross-examined by Potter's lawyer. Even the counsel for the prosecution seemed put off, but was content to say nothing. Soon he stood up, made a brief closing statement, and rested his case.

A groan escaped from poor Muff Potter, and he put his face in his hands and rocked softly to and fro, while a painful silence blanketed the courtroom. Many women began to sob. Counsel for the defense rose, and said:

"Your honor, in our remarks at the beginning of the trial, we intended to prove that our client did this fearsome deed while under a blind delirium caused by strong drink. We would like this opportunity to change our minds. We will not offer this plea. Call Tom Sawyer as a witness!"

A puzzled amazement awoke in every face in the house, including Potter's. Every eye fastened upon Tom as he rose and took his place on the stand. Tom's heart was pounding and there was a singing in his ears, for he was extremely scared. The oath was administered.

"Thomas Sawyer, where were you on the seventeenth of June, on or about the hour of midnight?"

Tom glanced at Joe's iron face, his cruel eyes, and words failed him. The audience listened breathless, but his words refused to come out. However, he got a part of his strength back, and put enough of it into his voice to be heard to at least the front rows:

"In the graveyard."

"A little louder, please. Don't be afraid."

"In the graveyard."

A contemptuous smile flitted across Injun Joe's face.

"Were you anywhere near Hoss Williams's grave?"

"Yes, sir."

"Just a trifle louder, son. How near were you?"

"Near as I am to you."

"Were you hidden?"

"I was."

"Where?"

"Behind the elms at the edge of the grave."

Injun Joe lost his smile and he continued to stare at Tom.

"Was there anyone else with you?"

"Yes, sir, I—"

"Never mind mentioning your companion's name. We will produce him at the proper time. Did you carry anything with you?"

Tom hesitated and looked confused.

"Speak out, my child. Don't be diffident. What did you take there?"

"Only a-a dead cat."

There was a brief ripple of mirth that died quickly away.

"Now, my boy, tell us everything that occurred. Tell it in your own way—don't skip anything, and don't be afraid."

Tom began to speak, hesitating at first, but as he warmed up, the words flowed more and more easily. In a little, every sound had ceased in the courtroom but his own voice; every eye was fixed on him; the audience hung on his every word, taking no note of time, or hunger, or discomfort. The pent emotion reached its climax when the boy said:

"—and as the doctor fetched Muff with the board, Injun Joe jumped forward with the knife and—"

Joe snarled and sprang to his feet, coming forward like a hungry wolf, and he was just within a few feet of Tom when

Mr. Branson produced a small pistol from the confines of his sling and shot him in the midsection, stopping the advance and almost assuredly saving Tom's life. In the next second, Joe clutched his bleeding stomach, sprang through a window—shattering the glass—and was gone!

24

Days of Splendor

Tom was a glittering hero once more—the pet of the old, and the envy of the young. His name even went into print, for the village paper ran an article on the trial of Muff Potter and Tom's subsequent exploits. There were those who believed he was destined for greatness, and could even be president one day, should he escape hanging. Mr. Branson, who had fired the shot that halted Injun Joe's attack, called Tom "a fine young lad . . . who's going to do us all proud, one way or t'other." It was Tom's unspoken belief that the old man could, in some way, not stop blaming himself for one unguarded moment of falling asleep in the sun, and this was the result. But it was nice to have an adult who was so undeniably *for* him. Aunt Polly supported the boy, but quietly, and in her own way. Mr. Branson had become Tom's political campaign manager, but if it didn't embarrass him, it certainly didn't embarrass Tom.

As usual, the fickle, unreasoning world took Muff Potter to its bosom for perhaps much the same reason. The villagers fondled him lavishly and were amused by the same actions that had once put them off. This sort of conduct is to the world's credit; therefore it would not be gracious to find fault with it. Muff was out of jail, a free man once more, and was not looking at the gallows in his immediate future. It was all he had ever wanted.

Tom's days were filled with admiration and splendor, but his nights were seasons of horror. Injun Joe infested his dreams and ruined his sleep, always with doom in his eye and a large, black dog at his beckoning. Some nights Tom would see the black dog in his dreams and pull himself out of sleep in anticipatory horror, for whenever he saw the black dog, Joe was only moments behind. Hardly any temptation could persuade the boy to roam abroad after nightfall. Joe could be waiting in the shadows, and this would be no dream. There could be no escape. Poor Huck was in the same state of agitation, for Tom had told the whole story to the lawyer the night before the great day of the trial, and Huck was sure his share of the business might leak out yet. Since Tom's battered conscience had managed to drive him to the lawyer's house and tell the story that had been presumably locked and sealed with the dismalest and most formidable of oaths, Huck's confidence in the human race was just about obliterated.

Half the time Tom was afraid that Injun Joe would never be captured; the other half he was afraid he would be. He was sure he would never draw a safe breath again until the man was dead and he had personally seen the corpse, and the accompanying head.

Rewards for Joe had been offered, but no Joe had been found. Some said that Mr. Branson's shot had hit him squarely in the vitals, and that Joe only escaped to die a lingering, painful death in some desolate hideout. If this were the case, everyone knew what the outcome would be. However, Mr. Branson was not entirely confident of his shot, and told his friends in secret that the bullet might have just grazed the flesh. In this case, some rest and a few changes of bandages, and Joe would be fine. Mr. Branson had occasion to worry here, himself. Joe was a vengeful man, and if he came back to punish Tom for his actions, it would make sense that he would come back for Mr. Branson, too.

A detective came up from St. Louis, moused around, and found some traces of blood on the window Joe had leapt through. He also found traces of blood in the bushes outside the court, and on a path leading down to the river. It was the detective's theory that Joe had taken passage and gone downriver. It was his educated guess—not knowing Joe—that Tom's little village was too "hot" for a scoundrel like that, and that he would continue to stir up mischief elsewhere in the future. Everyone believed this theory because it pleased everyone to believe it. Tom wanted to believe it most of all, but he still felt as insecure as he did before.

The slow, warm days drifted on, and each one left behind it a slightly lessened state of dread and apprehension. Aunt Polly promised Tom that his dreams would fade, and Tom wanted to believe her too.

25

The Search for Treasure

There is a time in every boy's life when he has a raging desire to go somewhere and dig for hidden treasure. This desire manifested itself in Tom only a few weeks into his latest notoriety, when it had cooled from a white-hot to a dull red. He sallied out to find someone to help him find this treasure and presently stumbled into Huck Finn the Red-Handed. Huck's part in Muff's trial had so far not been divulged, and so Huck was open to the enterprise. Huck was always willing to take a hand in anything that offered entertainment and required no capital, for he had a superabundance of the sort of time which is not money. "Where'll we dig?" said Huck.

"Oh, most anywhere."

"Why, is it hid all around?"

"No, indeed it ain't. It's hid in some mighty peculiar

places—sometimes on an island, sometimes in rotting chests under the limb of an old dead tree—but more often under the floorboards of haunted houses."

"Who hides it?"

"Why, robbers, of course—who'd you reckon? Sunday school teachers?"

"I don't know. If 'twas mine, I wouldn't hide it at all. I'd spend it and have a gay old time."

"So would I. But robbers ain't that way. They hide a treasure and leave it there, and sometime they come back. Or they don't come back at all—they die, and it just stays there till someone else finds it."

"Well, we've tried Jackson's Island a little, and we should try it again sometime; there's the haunted house up the Still-House branch, and there's plenty of dead-limbed trees."

"Then we should start as soon as possible. It could be anywhere. We'll have to go for all of 'em."

"Why, Tom, it'll take all summer!"

"So, what of it? Suppose you find a brass pot filled with a hundred silver coins in it, or a rotten wooden chest full of di'monds. How'd that be?"

Huck's eyes glowed.

"That'd be fine with me. Where do you propose we dig first?"

"Well, I don't rightly know. S'pose we tackle that old dead-limbed tree the other side of Still-House branch."

"Sounds bully to me."

So they obtained a pick and a shovel and set off on a three-mile tramp. They arrived hot and panting, and they threw themselves down in the shade of a neighboring elm to rest and have a smoke. It was a perfect day without clouds, adult supervision, or the undead.

"I like this," said Tom.

"So do I."

"Say, Huck, if we do find a treasure here, what're you going to do with your share?"

"My *share*?"

"Your half."

"Well, I'll have pie and a glass of soda every day and I'll go to every circus that comes along. If I hear of a circus that's only going to come nearby, I'll rent a carriage and go to it."

"Ain't you going to save any of it?"

"Save it? What fer?"

"Oh golly, so as to have something to live on, by and by."

"Ah, what good would that be? Pap would come to town some day and get his claws in it and clean me out pretty quick. What you goin' to do with yours, Tom?"

"I'm going to buy me a new drum, a real sword, a red necktie, maybe a good ol' pup, and get married."

"Married!"

"That's it."

"Tom—you—why, you ain't in your right mind."

"Wait, you'll see."

"Well, that's the craziest thing you could ever do. Look

at Pap and my mother. Fight? Why, they'd fight all the time. I remember, mighty well."

"That ain't nothin'. The girl I'm goin' to marry won't fight."

"What's the name of this gal?"

"Maybe I'll tell you sometime—but not now."

"Don't tell me then, but I think I could guess. Joe Harper told me you're always looking at her in class, and so did some of the other boys. Becky Thatcher."

Tom cringed. He thought he had been so careful, so demure, so cautiously discreet. "Why do you say her?"

" 'Cause it seems you turn into a fool in front of her."

"I do not. I just enjoy her company."

"Fine. But it's her, right?"

"You won't tell a soul?"

"Nah. Some of us are men of our word." The barb flew safely over Tom's head. "Besides, they already know."

"Then, yes, it's her. Becky Thatcher. I aim to marry her."

Huck thought about it from several angles. "All right. All right. That'll do. Only once you get married, I'll be more lonesome than ever."

"No, you won't. You'll come and live with me."

Huck brightened. "And I wouldn't be obliged to stay if I felt so inclined—I could come and go."

"You could do whatever you wanted to do."

"I could go for that."

"Sure, Becky wouldn't mind. She thinks you're fine. We'd give you your own room to keep your stuff in, and you'd come and go as you pleased. There'd always be a place at the table."

"Becky didn't agree to any of this, did she?"

"No, but I don't think she'd care. I know her. Now get up and let's get to diggin'."

They worked and sweated for a half hour. No result. They worked another half hour, and there was still nothing. Water began to come up in the hole. Huck said:

"Do they always bury it this deep?"

"Sometimes—not always. I reckon we haven't picked out the right spot."

So they chose a new spot and began digging again. The labor dragged a little, but still they made progress. Finally, Huck leaned on his shovel, admitted defeat, and said:

"Where do we dig next, Tom, after we give up on this one?"

"I reckon we'll tackle the old tree that's over yonder on Cardiff Hill, back of the widow's house."

"But won't the widow take it from us? It's on her land."

"*She* take it away? Maybe she'd like to try and take it. Whoever finds one of these hidden treasures, it belongs to them. Don't make no difference whose land it's on. It never was theirs in the first place."

That made sense, and the work went on. By and by, Huck said:

"Blame it, I believe we dug in the wrong place again. What do you think?"

Tom wiped his brow. "What a blamed lot of fools we are.

You're supposed to find out where the shadow of the branch falls at midnight, during a moon—not the middle of day. That's where you dig."

"Midnight? Ain't you worried about Joe?"

"Ah, he's gone away. He ain't ever comin' back here."

"So you can get out?"

"I bet I will. We've got to do it tonight, too, because if anyone else sees these holes we dug, they'll know in a second what we're up to here."

"Then let's stop for now. I'll come to your house later and stand under your window. I'll call like a tanager."

"I don't know the tanager. Kin you do the eastern thrush?"

Huck shook the dirt from his hands and put them on his hips. "In my sleep!"

The boys got together that night at the appointed time. Going on an adventure with Huck was much better than sleeping. There was almost no chance that the two of them would stumble into Injun Joe in the darkness, but it was an absolute certainty Tom would run into him in his dreams. By and by, they judged that midnight had come, they picked a spot, and began to dig. The hole deepened, and deepened further, but every time their pick or shovel struck something, it was only a stone or a chunk. At last, Tom said:

"It ain't no use, Huck. We're wrong again."

"It can't be wrong! Tom, we waited till midnight."

"I know, but there's another thing."

"What's that?"

"Why, we only guessed at the time. What if they buried it a little early, or a little late?"

Huck dropped his shovel. "That's it, then. We got to give this thing up. This time of night, with witches and ghosts littering around and such, I feel like somethin's behind me all the time. I've been kind of creepin' ever since we got here."

"I'm pretty much the same, Huck. And they most always put in a dead man when they bury a treasure, to keep guard over it."

"Lordy! So even if we do find the right spot, some Zum's goin' to rise up and try and scare us off! Ghosts and witches are one thing, Tom, a Zum is another. All a ghost can do is scare you outta your skin. A Zum can rise up and strike you down, kill you deader than dead! I'd rather have all the ghosts in the world after me over some angry Zum."

Tom had an inspiration. "I got it! The haunted house. They'll be treasure in that, for sure. And here's the kicker. Ghosts only travel about at night. They won't bother us at all in the daylight. We'll come back at noon!"

Huck was awestruck with the ingeniousness of it.

"So we just come back in the middle of the day. Perfect. There won't be anyone else there either—no one wants to go where a man's been murdered. We'll have the place to ourselves!"

They gathered themselves up and headed back to quiet civilization. On the way back, they passed the haunted house, utterly deserted, its fences torn apart by the Zum, the chimney crumbled into ruin, a corner of the roof caved in. The boys gazed a moment, half expecting to see ghostly blue lights floating past the windows. With this in mind, they gave the house a wide berth for now and made their way home, resolving to continue their treasure hunt in the brightness of the following morning.

26

The Haunted House

About noon the next day, the boys arrived at the dead tree
to retrieve their tools. All was as they had left it—the tools
were there, the deep and empty holes were there—but
their resolve had dissolved. They cast a judgmental eye on
the haunted house and decided to meet again, even earlier
in the morning, the following day. Ghosts evaporated at
dawn and came out again at dusk, or shortly thereafter. By
arriving earlier in the morning, it would give them several
more hours to search for treasure before an expeditious
departure.

On Saturday, early, the boys were at the dead tree again.
They had a smoke and a chat in the shade, and dug one
final hole, not with great hope, but merely because Tom
said that there were so many cases where people had given
up on a treasure after getting within inches of it, and then

someone else would come along and turn it up with a single, halfhearted thrust of a shovel. They failed at the final hole, and went away feeling not that they had trifled with fortune, but had fulfilled all the requirements that went into the business of treasure hunting.

When they reached the haunted house there was something so weird and grisly about the dead silence that reigned, and something so depressing about the loneliness and desolation of the place, that they were afraid for a moment to venture in. The house had been owned by a riverboat captain, a handsome, rugged young man who was on the verge of being enormously rich and prosperous. He had a wife and small child, and he went away for a week or two at a time, going up and down the river, while his energetic young wife supervised the building of a magnificent mansion, and saw to the care of their young son. Every time the captain returned, there was a wonderful new addition to the house that had been arranged and completed in his absence. New windows had been installed, a large and elaborate vegetable garden had been planted, a new slate roof had been put on. And always, his wife and son would meet him as he entered the gate, and he felt himself to be the richest and most fortunate man in the world.

On one particular autumn morning, he arrived home and his house was empty; no one met him at the gate. The windows were shuttered, the tomatoes were hanging on the vine, and the front yard had recently been swept of leaves, but the house was empty, locked, and dark. His wife had taken a carriage to buy paint and shingles for a new gazebo she had imagined, and a Zum had startled the horses, throwing them into a frenzy. The horses trampled the Zum, but drove the carriage into a shallow ditch, where it upended and killed both the captain's wife and son. It had happened just two days before his return. The captain put on a brave face and endured the ceremonies that followed, but became a broken man. He turned to drink, deteriorated rapidly, and ended his life soon after in the kitchen with a bullet to the head. The house had stood vacant ever since, partly because of the superstitious prejudices of the villagers, and partly because no one knew who the next of kin was in order to "bequeath" the cursed property and fill it with new faces.

Tom and Huck crept to the door and took a trembling look. They saw a dust-covered room filled with cloth-draped furniture; a cold, majestic fireplace; many broken windows; a beautiful and neglected staircase; and here, there, and everywhere, ragged and abandoned cobwebs. They presently entered, softly, with quickened pulses, talking in whispers, muscles tense and ready for immediate retreat. They were not familiar with the former tenants in their lifetime, and could only imagine the misery of the spirits who roamed the place after dark.

In a bit, familiarity modified their fears and they gave the place a critical and bold examination, admiring their own bravery. Next they decided to climb the staircase and examine the upstairs living area. In a way, this meant cutting off retreat, as there was only one way up and one way down, but they began to dare each other, and of course there could be only one result. They threw their tools into a dusty corner and made the ascent. Up on the second floor they found the same signs of decay. In one room they found a neglected closet that promised mystery, but the promise was a fraud, and they discovered nothing. Their courage was strong now and well in hand. They were about to go back downstairs when—

"Sh!" Tom said.

"What is it?" whispered Huck, blanching in fright.

"Sh . . . ! There . . . ! Hear it?"

"Yes! Oh my. Let's get out of here!"

"Keep still! Don't you move. They're moving around downstairs."

The boys flattened themselves upon the floor with their eyes to knotholes in the planking, and lay waiting in a misery of fear.

"They've stopped—no—they're coming! Don't whisper another word, Huck. My goodness, I wish I was out of here."

Two men entered the room below them. One was the old disabled Spaniard who hung around town and did menial jobs. The other they'd never seen before, a ragged, unkempt creature with nothing very pleasant about his face. When they came in, the unpleasant man was talking in a low voice; the two sat on the cloth-covered chairs and continued their remarks. The unpleasant one made a number of pained grimaces and pulled a wad of bloody bandages from his stomach and threw them to the floor.

Tom froze in utter panic.

The Spaniard said: "I've thought it over and I don't like it. It's far too dangerous."

"Dangerous!" grunted the unpleasant one, gasping for breath, and the boys immediately recognized the voice. It was Injun Joe. The boys fell into despair and began to cringe and quake. Injun Joe was on the floor below them. There was silence for some time. Then Joe said:

"It's no more dangerous than that other job up yonder—and nothin' came of that!"

"I know, I know. But things've changed. You're being looked for, for one thing. You need to stop movin' around so you can heal up proper. And I want to quit this place—it gives me the creeps. I wanted to yesterday, only there warn't no use trying to stir out of here with those infernal boys out there on the hill in plain view."

"Those infernal boys" quaked again with this remark, and wished in their hearts that they had confined their pirating to Jackson's Island.

The two men got out some food and made a luncheon.

"Does it hurt much?" the confederate asked Joe.

"Look here, lad—don't you worry about me. It hurts plenty, but I'm stronger than it is. It'll heal one way or t'other. You go back upriver where you belong and wait till you hear from me. When you do, bring the others. I'll stay here and get the look of things, and then we'll do one more job before we leg it down to Texas."

This was satisfactory to both of them. They finished eating, and presently, both men fell to yawning. Joe's comrade asked if he needed any more bandages, and Joe laughed derisively and said the whole first floor was covered with bandages.

First one, then both of them began to snore.

The boys drew a long and grateful breath.

"Now's our chance—let's get!"

Huck said:

"I can't, Tom. I'd die if they was to move."

Tom urged, but Huck held back. At last, Tom rose slowly and moved down the hall. He started down the staircase, but the first step he made wrung such a hideous creak that he sank down and stopped moving. It was a good thing, too. Joe sat up downstairs, stared ahead, listening, and kicked the other awake with his foot.

"Here! I thought you was watchin'!"

"Hey! Have I been asleep?"

"Oh, mostly, mostly. Nearly time for us to be movin', pard. What'll we do with what little swag we've got left?"

"I don't know—leave it as we've always done, I reckon. No use to take it away till we head south. Six hundred and fifty in silver is somethin' to carry."

"Right. We'll leave it. And bury it—deep."

"Good idea," said Joe's companion, who walked across the room, raised one of the loosened stones in the hearth, and took out a bag that jingled pleasantly. He took out a small handful for himself and another one for Joe, who was on his knees in the corner, digging at a spot of bare earth with his Bowie knife.

The boys forgot all their fears and miseries in an instant.

With gloating eyes, they watched Joe dig his hole. The splendor of it was beyond all imagination. Here was treasure hunting under the happiest of circumstance—there would not be any bothersome uncertainty as to where to dig. Tom and Huck nudged each other frequently—elegant nudges that were easily understood, they simply meant: "Oh, but ain't we glad we're here!"

Joe's knife struck something.

"Hello!" said he.

"What is it?" inquired his comrade.

"Oh, now. Wait. It's a box, I believe. Never mind, I've broke a hole."

He reached his hand in and drew it out.

"Man, it's money!"

The two men examined a handful of coins. They were all gold. The boys above were as excited as the men downstairs, though much quieter.

Joe's comrade said:

"I saw an old pick on the other side of the fireplace," and went to retrieve it.

He brought over the boys' pick and shovel. Injun Joe took the pick, muttering something to himself, then began to use it, occasionally wincing in pain as the wound in his midsection began to bleed anew. The box was soon unearthed. It was not very large. They pulled it out of its hole and opened it, contemplating the treasure awhile in blissful silence.

"Pard, there's thousands of dollars here," said Joe.

" 'Twas always said that the captain who lived here died with money," his comrade replied.

"And I believe we've found it," said Joe.

"Now we can skedaddle to Texas and you won't have to do that last job."

Injun Joe frowned. He said:

"Then you don't know me so well as that. 'Twasn't robbery, altogether—it's revenge! And I'll be needin' your help in it. Then, when it's all finished, off we go to Texas."

"If you say so. What'll we do with all this—bury it again?"

"Yes." (Profound delight overhead.) "But not here." (Equally profound distress overhead.) "I've had my fill of this place, too. Why leave it here and have to return for yet another performance? No—we'll take it back to my den and bury it there."

"Why of course! I never thought of that before. You're in Number One?"

"No—Number Two—the one under the cross."

"All right. Let's get this swag out of here."

Joe got up, limping a little as he moved, and went about from window to window, peeping out cautiously. He grumbled to himself for a while, not seeming to be taken by his good fortune, but finally he wrapped a length of white linen around his wound and commanded his comrade to pick up his side of the metal box. They slipped out of the house in the deepening twilight and moved toward the river.

Tom and Huck rose up, weak but vastly relieved not to have been discovered, and stared at the two retreating figures between unfilled chinks in the house. Follow them? Was that the next step? No, not then. The hour was too late, their quarry too alert for danger, too suspicious, too evil.

A ghastly thought occurred to Tom.

"He mentioned revenge. What if he means us, Huck?"

"Oh, Lord!" said Huck, almost fainting.

They talked it all over, and as they returned to the village, they agreed to believe that Joe probably meant revenge on someone else—or at least he meant revenge on nobody but Tom, since only Tom had testified at the trial. It was small comfort for Tom to be alone in danger. Huck's company would be a marked improvement, he thought. But there were too many other things to think about. They left each other for the night, both of them hopelessly lost in thought. If a Zum had crossed their path, they might not have noticed it.

27

Doubts to Be Settled

The adventure of the day mightily invaded Tom's dreams that night. The dream seemed to repeat itself. Each time he and Huck were in the haunted house; they found a spot and dug for hidden treasure; four times they found it and pulled it out of the ground; four times Tom heard a cry and whirled around to see Injun Joe before them, his wounds magically healed, stronger than ever. Four times the treasure vanished in his fingers as sleep forsook him and wakefulness brought back the cold reality of his misfortune. By daybreak, he lay in bed exhausted, and it seemed the incidents of his great adventure were curiously subdued and far away—something that had happened in another world, or in a time long gone by. Then it occurred to him that the great adventure itself had been a dream. There was one strong argument in favor of this idea—namely, that the quantity of coins he had seen was too vast to be real. He had never seen as much as fifty dollars in one chunk before, and imagined that all references to "hundreds" and "thousands" were mere fanciful expressions invented by grown-ups, and that no such sums really existed in real life. He had never believed for a moment that so large a sum as a hundred dollars could be found in anyone's possession. When he thought about the handsome young river captain and his circumstances, it made the tragedy seem infinitely greater. If Tom's notion of buried treasure had been analyzed, it would have consisted of a handful of real coins and a bushel of vague, splendid, ungraspable dollars. For the first time in his life, he had the idea that true wealth was more than he had ever imagined, and more than he could imagine. It made the world seem a larger place than it had been the day before.

He snatched a quick breakfast without chatting with Aunt Polly and went to find Huck. Huck was sitting on the gunwale of a flatboat, listlessly dangling his feet in the water and looking very melancholy.

"Hello, Huck."

"Hello yourself."

Silence for a minute.

"Tom, think how close we came to finding that treasure for ourselves. We'd have the money right now, instead of Joe. And now it's gone!"

" 'Tain't a dream, then. 'Tain't a dream. I woke up this morning and wondered if I made up the whole thing. I almost wish I had."

"What ain't a dream?"

"Oh, yesterday. The box of gold. I was half thinking it was."

"Dream! If them two had decided to come upstairs and wander around a bit, you'd 'a seen how much dream it was! I've had me some dreams of my own—with that evil-eyed Joe going after me all through it."

"Was there a dog?"

"Was there *where* a dog?"

"In your dream—a big, black dog that followed Joe around? I dream of Joe most every night, and he always seems to have a big black Zum dog with him. Joe was in my dreams, but there warn't no black dog last night. Thought he might be in yours."

"No, thank you. It was just Joe by himself . . . Tom, I feel miserable. We'll never find it now. A fella don't have but one chance for a pile like that—and we had the chance, and it's gone. We'll never find another one."

"Then what if we track Joe and find him? We track Joe, we find the treasure."

"We'll never find him. I'd feel mighty shaky if we was to see him, anyway."

"Well, me too. But if we could track him back to his Number Two, we'd know where the treasure was."

"Number Two—yes, that's what he said. Number Two. I been thinkin' about that. But I can't make nothin' out of it. What do you reckon it is?"

"I dunno. Say, Huck, maybe it's the number of a house!"

Huck shook his head. "Nah, that id'n it. If it is, it ain't in this town. There ain't no numbers here."

"Well, that's so. Lemme think a minute. Here—it could be the number of a room—like in a tavern, you know?"

"Oh, that's the trick. I like it. And there ain't but two taverns. We can find out quick!"

"You stay here, Huck, till I come back."

Tom, who did not care to have Huck's company under the circumstances, was off at once, on the lookout for Zum along the way. He found that in the nicer tavern, a young lawyer occupied the number two room, and had been living there for several months. In the less ostentatious tavern, number two was a bit of a mystery. The tavernkeeper's son said that the number two room was kept locked all the time, and he almost never saw anyone come in or go out of it except at night. He did not have a powerful curiosity about this state of things, because there were many things about tavern life that were not usual. But he remembered that he had seen a light under the door the night before.

Tom reported back to Huck in less than an hour, and told him he had found the Number Two they had been looking for.

"I reckon it is, Tom. Now what do you propose we do?"

Tom thought about it a long time. Then he said:

"I'll tell you what. The back door of that room comes out onto an alley between the tavern and an old brick building. You go round up all the door keys you can find, and I'll nip all of Aunt Polly's, and the first dark night, we'll go and try 'em all. Until then, mind you, keep an eye out for Injun Joe, because he might be about, spying and looking for a chance to get his revenge. If you see him, get in behind him and follow him—if he don't wind up at Number Two, we've got the wrong place."

"Lordy, I don't want to foller him by myself."

"Why, it'll be night. He won't even see you—and if he does, maybe he won't even think anything."

"I dunno. I dunno. I guess I'll try."

"He'll lead you to that hidden treasure."

"It's so, Tom, it's so. I'll do it! I will!"

"Now you're talking, Huck! Keep your eyes open, and we'll have another chance at this treasure yet. Don't you ever weaken, Huck. I won't either."

28

An Attempt at the Treasure

That night Tom and Huck were ready for their adventure. They hung around the neighborhood of the tavern until after nine, one watching the alleyway at a distance and the other keeping an eye on the tavern door. No one entered the alley or left it, and no one resembling Injun Joe entered or left the tavern. The night promised to be clear and un-cloudy, so Tom went home with the understanding that if a considerable amount of darkness came on, Huck was to come for him. The night, however, remained clear and Huck finally returned to bed in an empty molasses barrel around midnight.

The next several evenings were similarly uneventful, but Thursday night promised better. The sky was full of dark clouds that threatened rain and obliterated the moon. Tom slipped out of the house with his aunt's old tin lantern, and borrowed a large towel to blindfold it with. An hour before midnight, the tavern closed up and its lights (the only ones thereabouts) were put out. Neither Joe nor his confederate had been seen. An inky blackness covered everything, and the stillness was interrupted only by occasional rumblings of distant thunder.

Tom took the lantern, wrapped it closely in the towel, and the two adventurers crept in the gloom toward the tavern. Huck stood sentry while Tom felt his way down the alley. Huck soon wished he could see a flash from the lantern—anything that would tell him that Tom was still alive. It seemed hours since Tom had disappeared. Perhaps he had fainted; maybe he was dead. Huck found himself fearing all sorts of dreadful things. Suddenly, there was a brief noise and a flash of light, and Tom came running by him:

"Run!" he said; "Run for your life!"

Tom did not need to repeat it; once was enough. Both boys flew, never stopping till they reached the shed of a deserted slaughterhouse at the lower end of town. Just as they arrived, the heavens opened and the rain began to pour. As soon as they could catch their breath, Tom said:

"Huck, it was awful! I tried a few of the keys we brought, but each one clattered in the lock and made such a racket I could scarcely breathe! None of 'em would turn in the lock, neither. Well, without noticin' much what I was doin', I took hold of the knob, and—what do you know—open comes the door! It warn't locked. I came in, took the towel off the lantern, and great Caesar's ghost!"

"What'd you see, Tom?"

"Huck, I almost stepped on Joe's hand! I think I did step on his hand."

"No!"

"Yes! He was laying there, flat out on the floor with his arms all splayed out—dead to the world!"

"Lordy, what did you do? Did he wake up?"

"No, never moved even a tiny bit. Seemed a little curious, because I was pretty sure I stepped on his hand—it was dark, see. I couldn't tell. Anyways, he didn't move, didn't stir, wasn't doin' no snorin' either; nothing; I never seen anyone sleep like that. Even Aunt Polly sleeps lighter than that, and she can sleep through a lot. He was either finally dead from the gunshot wound, or drunker'n anyone I've ever seen."

"Pap does that. He always sleeps like the dead, though with him, it's the cider. Say, Tom, did you see the box?"

"Huck, I didn't want to look around. I just glanced, and I didn't see no box, and I didn't see no cross. I didn't see anything but a bunch of bottles strewn 'round the room."

"You know, Tom, now might be a mighty good time to get that box, if ol' Joe's drunk."

"Oh, I think you're right, Huck, but even flat out on the ground, he scares me."

"Me too. But if he's as out as you say, now's the best time. When Pap gets that kind of drunk, you could beat on a drum and not roust him. He'd still be out by the next afternoon."

In a few minutes when the rain eased up, the two boys

set off for a repeat visit to the darkened tavern. They were bolder this time, for Huck had convinced them both that Joe had drunk himself senseless with alcohol. But when they got to the alley, they heard sudden footsteps approaching them, and hid behind a wooden crate. Joe had come out of his room and was walking briskly to the end of the alleyway and into the ensuing darkness. It was not a drunkard's walk, and both boys thought it was curious that he was no longer walking like a man who had been recently shot in the stomach with a pistol. When he had disappeared, Tom and Huck were compelled to check the room for the metal box. There was none. What they did find was an assortment of empty bottles, a few full ones, and a floor slick with fresh blood and strewn with piles of filthy bandages. It was enough for them. They both beat a hasty retreat.

Far, far away from the gory scene, they agreed to continue watching the room, with the expectation that Joe would sooner or later bring the metal box back to have it close to him. Huck agreed to watch the room for as long as it took—if Tom agreed to come back and snatch the box at the first opportunity. Both boys agreed to their parts of the contract.

"I'm goin' home for now, Huck. Something happens and Joe brings that box back, you come get me. If I'm asleep, you know how to wake me up."

"I said I would and I will. I'll watch that tavern every night for a year! More! I'll sleep all day and watch every night."

"And if I don't need you in the daytime, I'll let you

sleep," Tom said. "I won't come bothering around. Anytime you see somethin's up, in the night, just come around and wake me."

"Common thrush still okay?" Huck asked.

Tom thought about it. "Was that what you was last time?"

Huck could not remember. "I think," he said.

"Then keep it the same. Whichever you're doin', it wakes me up."

29

The Picnic

The first thing Tom heard on Friday was that Judge Thatcher's family had come back into town the night before. Both Joe and the box of treasure sank into secondary importance, and Becky took the chief place in the boy's interest. He went to see her and had an exhausting good time playing with her and a crowd of their schoolmates. The day was crowned with great news: Becky's mother announced that the long-promised and long-delayed picnic would be the following day. The invitations went out before sunset, and straightaway the young people of the village were thrown into a fever of preparation and pleasurable anticipation. Tom's excitement kept him awake until a pretty late hour, for he had hoped to surprise Becky and the other picnickers with the box of treasure, but no signal came that night from Huck. He was disappointed.

Morning came, and by ten o'clock, a giddy and rollicking company was gathered at Judge Thatcher's, and everyone was ready for a start. It was not the custom of elderly people to mar picnics with their presence. The children were considered safe enough under the wings of a few young ladies of eighteen, and a few more young gentlemen of about twenty-three who carried rifles and were confident shots. The old steam ferryboat was chartered for the occasion, and the company filed on board with provision baskets. Sid was sick and had to miss the fun, and Mary stayed home to entertain him. The last thing Mrs. Thatcher said to Becky was:

"You won't be back till late. Perhaps you'd better stay all night with some of the girls that live near the ferry landing, child."

"Then I'll stay with Susy Harper, Mother."

"Very good. Remember to behave yourself and don't be any trouble."

Presently, as they walked to the ferry, Tom said:

"Say—I'll tell you what we'll do. Instead of goin' to the Harpers, we'll climb up the hill and stop at the Widow Douglas's. She'll have ice cream. She has it most every day—and she'll be awful glad to have us."

Becky reflected a moment and said:

"But what will my mother have to say?"

"Aww, how'll she know? She *won't* know, so what's the harm? All she wants is that you'll be safe—and the Douglas place is the safest place in town. It's like a fort. Better."

The Widow Douglas's splendid hospitality was a tempting idea, and Tom's reasoning carried the day. So it was decided to say nothing to anyone about the night's program. It occurred to Tom that he wouldn't be available for Huck should tonight be the night he gave the signal, but the sure fun of the evening outweighed the possibility of treasure, and he thought of the box of money no more that day.

Three miles below town, the ferryboat stopped at the mouth of a hollow and tied up. The crowd swarmed ashore and soon the whole forest echoed with happy shouting and laughter. After the feast of the picnic, they rested in the shade of spreading oaks, and by and by someone shouted:

"Who's ready for the caves?"

Everyone was. Bundles of candles were procured, and there was a general scamper up the hill. The mouth of the cave was upon the hillside and had an opening shaped like the letter A. A massive oaken door stood welcoming at the entrance. Within was a small chamber, chilly as an icehouse, and walled with limestone that was dewy with a cold sweat. It was romantic and mysterious to stand in the deep gloom of the entrance and look out upon the green valley shining in the sun. By and by, the procession went filing down the steep descent of the main avenue, their candles revealing lofty walls of rock nearly sixty feet overhead. Every few steps another aisle branched out on either side, for the cave was in fact a vast labyrinth. It was said one might wander days and nights and still never find the end to the cave, for it was a confusing, unending maze of chambers and passageways. No one "knew" the whole cave, just little parts of it.

The procession moved along the main chamber some three-quarters of a mile, and then groups and couples began to slip into the side and branch avenues, popping out in surprise at their comrades where the corridors joined again. Groups were able to elude each other for a good deal of time without going beyond the "known" ground.

Little by little, one group after another came straggling back to the open mouth of the cave, panting, smeared from head to foot with candle drippings, daubed with clay, and they were astonished to find that they had lost all track of time and night was almost at hand. The clanging ferry bell had been calling for half an hour. However, this sort of close to the day was romantic and entirely satisfactory. The guards had seen nothing out of the ordinary, sensed nothing out of the ordinary, the children were all exhausted and happy, and no one cared about the wasted time but the captain of the boat.

Huck was already at his watch when the ferryboat lights came glinting past the wharf. He wondered briefly what boat it was, but soon dropped it from his mind and concentrated on the task at hand. The night was going to be increasingly cloudy and dark. Eleven o'clock came, the tavern lights were extinguished, and darkness settled everywhere. Huck watched a long time and even dozed a little. His faith in the adventure was beginning to unravel, and he wondered mournfully if the treasure was out of his hands for good.

He heard a noise coming from the alley. He was all attention in an instant. The alley door closed softly, and two men walked by him, and one seemed to have a small box under his arms. It was too late to go and retrieve Tom; the men were moving, and with purpose; they would disappear and never be found again. No, he would follow in their wake. So Huck stepped out and glided just behind the men, catlike, allowing them to keep just far enough ahead to not be visible.

They moved up the darkened street for three blocks, turned, and went straight ahead, until they came to the path that led up Cardiff Hill. They passed by the old Welshman's compound, halfway up the hill, and went on the summit. Huck shortened his distance now, for they would never be able to see him. He trotted on awhile, then slackened his pace, then stopped altogether and just listened. There was no sound, only the beating of his own heart. But he heard no more footsteps. He remained still. In the distance, he could see through the bushes to the reflection of one of the Widow Douglas's bonfires, and so knew he was close to one of the guard towers at the edge of her property.

Now there was a voice—a low, low voice—Injun Joe's:

"Are you all here?"

A number of men murmured in answer.

"Good. You all know the plan. We mean to take out the guards at the perimeter first, then everyone left inside will be easier pickins. Trapped. By dawn we'll have a command of the whole village. Remember—whosoever falls I will bring back again—stronger than before! Our numbers can only grow, while theirs dwindle!"

A deadly chill went to Huck's heart—this, then, was the job they had been talking about in the haunted house. His first thought was to fly. Then he remembered the Widow Douglas, who had been kind to him more than once. These men were going to murder her, and everyone in her employ. Huck had a disturbing revelation. Injun Joe had not gotten better from his wound at all. He should have realized this when they noticed all the blood on the floor of Joe's room. No, he had gotten worse, and died. Joe had turned into one of *them*, a Zum, but a kind Huck had never heard of before. The Zum he was familiar with did not speak, they did not reason, they did not want, and they did not plan. This was something new, something not seen before, and the idea was unfathomably dreadful. Joe was gathering about him an army of men who had been promised more than gold and silver and glorious victory. It was too much to think about at the present time. He wanted to be able to warn the Widow Douglas and her men, but he knew he did not dare—they would catch him, and make him one of *them*. He could not spit and tell them he would die first, as that was only the first step in the process.

He thought all of this and more in the moments before Joe's next remark:

"After we take and secure this compound, we'll break into groups, take down the telegraph wires, and just wreak mayhem. There will be fear and confusion, and in the confusion, we will press our advantage. If they flee, let them! If they stay and fight, we bring them down and bring them into our fold! Our numbers will grow like a small, dry forest hit by a single bolt of lightning. And you, my friends, will be the first!"

Another voice in the darkness said: "Well, if it's to be done, let's get to it. The quicker, the better. I'm all in a shiver."

"Now—do it now? Impatient are you? Look here—I'll get suspicious of you, first thing you know. No, we'll wait for the widow's bonfires to die down—there's no hurry yet. It won't be a long while."

Huck felt that a silence was going to ensue—a thing more awful than any more of this murderous Zum talk; so he held his breath and stepped gingerly back; he planted his foot carefully, and firmly, first on one side, then on the other. He repeated the procedure. After a dozen steps, he turned and stepped cautiously on. When he emerged at the edge of the stand of bushes, he felt more secure, and so he picked up his nimble heels and flew. Down, down he sped, till he reached the Welshman's compound. He banged on the door of his front gate and presently the heads of an old man and two of his stalwart sons were thrust from the windows.

"What's the row there? Who's banging? What do you want?"

"Let me in—quick. I'll tell everything!"

"Why, who are you?"

"Huckleberry Finn—quick, let me in!"

"Huckleberry Finn indeed! It ain't a name to open many doors, I judge. But let him in, boys, and we'll see what's the trouble."

The large front door was unbarred and opened.

"Please don't ever tell I told you," were Huck's first words when he got in. "Please don't—I'll be killed, sure— but the widow's always been good friends to me, and I want to tell—I *will* tell if you promise you won't let on that it was me."

"By George, he *has* got something important to say, or he wouldn't act so!" the old man exclaimed. "Out with it, lad, and no one here'll ever tell a word."

It was a fantastic tale, unbelievable, but Huck's state of sheer terror made them realize it was something true—an evil thing, and unwanted, yet something true. The old Welshman and his sons woke every able-bodied hand in the compound, armed them, and five minutes later a large, grim contingent of well-armed men was moving quietly up the hill. The old man even gave Huck a rifle and told him he hoped he knew how to use it. They moved forward in the darkness, moving ahead slowly. All of a sudden there was an explosion of firearms and a loud cry. The guards in the wooden towers began clanging an alarm bell, and other guards came out of a bunkhouse and began to pour buckets of kerosene onto the dying bonfires. The leaping flames illuminated a scene of mad confusion, terror, and bloodshed. During brief flashes of illumination, Huck saw Injun Joe rallying and cursing at his own men. His long, jagged shadow stretched across a darkened landscape. In an instant, Joe grabbed an attacker, crushed his throat, then lifted him above his head and threw him toward the advancing forces. His eyes seemed to burn like fiery embers in the darkness. Huck could not bear it; he discharged his weapon, threw it down, and ran.

30

Hope and Despair

At the first glimpse of dawn on Sunday morning, Huck came groping up the hill and rapped gently at the Welshman's door. Most everyone was exhausted and asleep, but it was a sleep that was set on a hair trigger, on account of the episode of the previous evening. A rifle barrel came through a slot and a voice shouted:

"Who's there?"

Huck's scared voice answered in a low tone:

"Please let me in! It's only Huck Finn!"

The door immediately was unbolted, and swung open. "It's a name that can open this door day or night, lad—and welcome!"

It was the strangest thing Huck had ever heard, and the most pleasant. He could not recall an instance where any-one had ever welcomed him before. The old man clasped

Huckleberry in a joyous hug and pounded him on the back before pulling him inside and bolting the door again.

"Now my boy, it was a grim night, but I hope you're good and hungry, because breakfast will be ready as soon as the sun's up. We'll have a piping hot one, too! We all hoped you'd turn up and stop here last night."

"I was awfully scared and I run," Huck admitted. "I took out when the pistols went off and I didn't stop for three miles. I've come here now because I want to know more about it, you know; and I came before it was daylight because I didn't want to run across them devils, especially them that were dead."

"Well my boy, you look as though you've had a bad night of it—but there's a bed here for you when you've had your breakfast. You were right to be cautious, as we didn't get them all, lad—we are sorry enough for that. We got within fifteen feet of them—dark as a cellar that sumac path was—and then I found I was going to sneeze. I was in the lead with my pistol raised, and when I sneezed, those scoundrels—most of them—knew what they were in for and began disappearing into the bushes. So I sang out, 'Fire, boys!' and blazed away at the place where the rustling was. So did the rest of us. Five or six fell down dead, and most of the rest of them went through the woods and I guess we never touched them. The leader and one or two others stayed and fought, and soon enough it was just he by himself. He kilt two of my men, and bashed one of my sons with a rifle butt, hurting him pretty bad—he's in the next room, being attended to. I believe he'll make it back to us with some attention and a lot of rest. But we overwhelmed the devil, and shot him several times before he disappeared with the rest, and we made an attempt to pursue. As soon as we lost the sound of their feet we quit chasing, and went back to where their fallen lay. They each got another slug in the head to put an end to that particular discussion. Then we went and stirred up the constables. They got a posse together and went off to beat up the woods, where I've just been told one or two more have thrown up their hands and surrendered. As soon as it's light out, the sheriff and a gang are going to walk the riverbank and see if we can find any more. One of my boys will be with them presently. I wished we had some sort of description of those rascals—'twould help a great deal. But you couldn't see what they was like in the dark, I suppose."

"Oh yes, I saw them downtown and follered them."

"Splendid! Describe them, my boy!"

"One was Injun Joe, and the other was a mean-lookin', ragged—"

"That's enough lad. So it *was* Joe—we know all about that devil. Me and a few men came on them in the woods in back of the widow's one day, and they slunk off. Warn't nothing to arrest them with, but it was awful suspicious. Now I begin to see what they were doin'."

Huck grabbed the Welshman by his wrists and exclaimed:

"Oh, please don't tell anyone it was me that blowed on them! Oh please!"

"All right, all right, if you say so, Huck, but you ought to get the credit for what you did."

"Oh, no, no. Please don't tell!"

The old Welshman said: "My sons won't. And I won't. But why don't you want it known?"

Huck would not explain, other than that it was Injun Joe, which seemed enough of an explanation, and that he put a lot of stock in Joe's sense of revenge, and less in his ability to be caught and brought to trial.

The old man promised secrecy once more, and said:

"How did you happen to follow them fellows, lad?"

Huck was silent while he framed a cautious reply. Then he said:

"Well, you see, I couldn't sleep. I can't hardly ever sleep. So I come along and go outside 'bout midnight, thinkin' I'll walk around at least till I get tired enough to lie down. I was in back by the tavern, and just then along come these two chaps with somethin' under their arm and I got the feelin' they stole it. So I followed them, all the way to just outside the widow's guard towers."

"Go on," the old man said. "I won't betray you."

"And I listened to them talk a bit, and when I got a handle on what they were fixin' to do, I came down and knocked on your door."

During breakfast, the talk went on, and in the course of it, the old man said that the last thing he had done after bringing his wounded son back to the compound and retiring for what remained of the night, was to get a lantern and go examine the area and make sure all of the scoundrels who were laid low had been properly dispatched to prevent them rising up again. They captured a bulky bundle of—

"Of what!?" Huck gasped.

The Welshman was startled by Huck's suddenness, and replied:

"Firearms, mostly. Pistols. Axes. Gunpowder. Joe's gang was not well-heeled on their own, and he must have gotten his hands on some armaments to make them a little more formidable. That appears to relieve you a great deal. What were you expecting we'd find?"

Huck was in a close place—he would have given anything for material to flesh out a plausible answer, but nothing suggested itself.

"Sunday school books, maybe?"

Poor Huck was too distressed to smile, but the old man laughed loud and joyously, and ended up saying that a good laugh was money in a man's pocket, because it cut the doctor's bills like anything. Then he added:

"Poor old chap. You're white and jaded—you've seen too much for one day. But you'll come out of it. God willing, my son, too. Rest and sleep will fetch you both all right, I think."

Huck was irritated that he had been such a goose and betrayed such a suspicious excitement, but on the whole he was glad it had happened, for now he knew beyond all question that the treasure had not been discovered, and so his mind was at rest and exceedingly comfortable.

Just as breakfast was completed, there was another knock on the door. The Welshman admitted several ladies and gentlemen, among them the Widow Douglas, and noticed that groups of citizens were climbing up the hill to examine the carnage. So the news was spreading.

The Welshman had to tell the story of the preceding night to his visitors. The widow's gratitude for her preservation was outspoken.

"Don't say a word about it, madam. There's another that you're more beholden to than you are to me and my boys, but he won't allow me to tell his name. We wouldn't have been there but for him."

More visitors came, and the story had to be told and retold for a few hours more.

There was no Sunday school during day-school vacation, but everyone was early at church to exchange bits of news. The event was well canvassed, as was the fact that Joe and his original comrade were still on the loose. When the sermon was finished, Judge Thatcher's wife sat down next to Mrs. Harper and said:

"Is my Becky going to sleep all day? I just expected she would be tired to death."

"Your Becky?"

"Our daughter—Becky," she said with a startled look. "Didn't she stay with you last night?"

"Why, no."

Mrs. Thatcher turned pale and sank into a pew, just as Aunt Polly, talking briskly with a friend, passed by. Aunt Polly said:

"Good morning, Mrs. Thatcher. Good morn, Mrs. Harper. I've a boy that's turned up missing. I reckon he's stayed at one of your homes last night. And now he's afraid to come to church. I've got to settle with him." She waved her axe handle menacingly, but everyone was familiar with her terrible, swift companion.

Mrs. Thatcher shook her head feebly and turned paler than ever.

"He didn't stay with us," said Mrs. Harper, beginning to feel uneasy. A marked anxiety came to Aunt Polly's face.

"Joe Harper, have you seen my Tom this morning?"

"No'm."

"When did you see him last?"

Joe tried to remember, but was not sure he could say. Other children were anxiously questioned, and the chaperones for the picnic were summoned. They said they had not noticed whether Tom and Becky were on board the ferryboat on the homeward trip; it was dark, and no one thought of inquiring if anyone was missing. One young man finally blurted out his fear that they were still in the cave! Mrs. Thatcher fainted dead away, and Aunt Polly fell to crying and wringing her hands.

The alarm went from lip to lip, from group to group, and soon the whole town was up. The Cardiff Hill episode sank into relative insignificance as most of the conspirators had been slain or were taken into custody. Horses were saddled, skiffs were manned, and before the horror was a half hour old, two hundred men were pouring down the road toward the cave.

All the rest of the day the village seemed deserted and quiet. That night the town waited for news, but when morning finally arrived, the only word that came was "Send more candles—send food." Judge Thatcher sent messages of encouragement and hope from the cave, but even he feared the worst.

The old Welshman came home at daybreak, spattered with candle grease, smeared in clay, and almost worn out. He found Huck still in the bed that had been provided for him, his son sleeping in another room, his wound wrapped in clean dressing. Huck was delirious with fever. The physicians were all at the cave, so the Widow Douglas came and took care of the wounded boys.

By the next afternoon, parties of defeated men began to struggle into the village, but the strongest of men continued searching. The only news that could be gained was that parts of the cave had been scoured and ransacked that had never been visited before; that wherever one wandered through the maze of passages, lights were seen flittering here and there in the darkness. In one place, far from the sections of the cave usually visited by the tourists, the names BECKY & TOM had been found traced on the ceiling in candle smoke, and nearby, a grease-soiled ribbon was found that Mrs. Thatcher recognized as her daughter's.

Three dreadful days it went on, and the village sank into a hopeless stupor.

In a lucid interval, Huck finally asked if anything had been found at Joe's room at the tavern.

"Yes," said the widow.

Huck sat up in bed, wild-eyed.

"What! What was it?"

"Liquor! Many, many bottles of liquor. Lie down, child. What a turn you gave me!"

"Was it Tom Sawyer who found it?"

The widow burst into tears. "Hush, hush, child, hush! I've told you before, you must not talk. You are very, very, very sick."

So the treasure had not been found. It was therefore gone forever. But Huck noticed the widow crying. Huck thought it curious that she should cry. She continued to cry, and Huck closed his eyes again and lapsed back into unconsciousness.

31

Lost in the Cave

Now to return to Tom and Becky at the picnic. They tripped along the murky aisles with the rest of the company, visiting the familiar wonders of the cave—wonders dubbed with rather over-descriptive names, such as "The Cathedral," "Aladdin's Palace," "The Drawing Room," and so on. Presently, the hide-and-seek frolicking began, and Tom and Becky engaged in it until it began to grow a trifle wearisome; they then wandered down a sinuous avenue holding their candles aloft and reading the webwork of names, dates, post-office addresses, and mottoes that had been frescoed upon the walls in candle smoke.

Presently they came to a place with a little stream of water. They followed the stream for a ways, and as they walked, Tom was seized with an ambition to be a discoverer and explorer. Periodically, they put a smoke mark on the wall for future guidance and continued on their quest. They wound their way deep down into the secret depths of the cave, made another mark, and continued, in search of novelties to tell the upper world about. In one place they found a spacious cavern, from whose ceiling descended a multitude of shiny stalactites, and presently left by one of the many passages that opened to it. This shortly brought them to a bewitching spring in what appeared to be an enormous room. The candles disturbed thousands of bats, and they came flocking down by the hundreds, wave after wave, squeaking and darting furiously at the candles. Tom grabbed Becky's hand and they plunged into any new passage that offered itself, until at last they were rid of the perilous things. Tom found a subterranean lake that he wanted to explore, but concluded it would be best to sit and rest awhile, first.

Now for the first time, the deep stillness of the place laid a clammy hand on the children's spirits. Becky said:

"Why, I didn't notice, but it seems ever so long since I heard any of the others. I wonder how long we've been down here, Tom. Perhaps we'd better start back."

"Yes, I reckon we'd better. But we'll have to find some other way to steer clear of those bats. If they put our candles out, we'd be in an awful fix."

Tom started through a corridor, glancing at each new opening to see if there was something familiar about it; but they were all strange. Each time Tom made an examination, Becky would watch his face for an encouraging sign, and he would say cheerily:

"Oh well! This ain't the one, but we'll come to it right away!"

But he was less and less hopeful with each failure, and began to turn into diverging avenues at sheer random, desperate to find a way out. He still said it was "all right" but the words began to lose their ring. Becky tried to hold back her tears, but they came anyway. At last she said:

"Oh Tom, never mind the bats, let's go back that way! We seem to get worse and worse all the time!"

Tom stopped, and he realized he could not find his way back. He had stopped making smoke marks on the walls. "Becky, I was such a fool! Such a fool! I never thought we might want to come back the same way. I can't find the way—it's all mixed up!"

"Tom, we'll never get out of this awful place, will we? Oh, why did we ever have to leave the others."

She sank to the ground and burst into such a frenzy of crying that Tom was appalled with the idea that she might die. He sat down with her and put his arms around her. She clung to him, and poured out her terror, her unavailing regrets, and the distant echoes of the place turned them all to jeering laughter. Tom begged her to pluck up hope again, but she could not. When they finally moved on, it was with leaden hearts, and they proceeded simply at random.

By and by Tom took Becky's candle and blew it out. Becky understood, but her hope failed even more. She knew he was trying to economize their candles before they ran out of light completely.

At last Becky's frail limbs refused to carry her any farther.

She sat down in a sprawl, and Tom rested with her, and they talked of home, and friends, and comfortable beds, and above all, the light! Tom tried to think of some way to comfort her, but all his encouragements were grown threadbare with use, and sounded like sarcasm. Fatigue bore so heavily upon Becky that she drifted off to sleep. Tom was grateful. He sat looking at her drawn face and saw it grow smooth and natural under the influence of pleasant dreams; and by and by a smile dawned and rested there. While he was deep in his own musings, Becky awoke with a breezy little laugh—but it was stricken dead, and a groan followed it.

"I'm glad you've slept, Becky. You had a good dream. I could tell. You'll feel rested now and we'll find the way out."

"I don't think so, Tom."

Silence.

"Will you tell me something, Becky?"

"Yes. Of course."

"You do love me, don't you? It's just you and me here. You can say it."

"Yes, Tom. Of course. I love you."

"And I love you. I never meant to hurt you before." He was referring to Amy Lawrence, but was smart enough not to repeat the mistake of mentioning her by name.

She grabbed his hands and held on tightly. "That all seems so long ago. I don't care. Not at all. But I think we should keep it a secret—just something between you and me. Please don't tell anyone else—I mean, if we—when—"

and she began to cry again. Tom was quiet and let her cry for a few minutes, then stood up.

"Let's keep trying," he said.

They rose up and wandered along, hand in hand, sad and without hope. They tried to figure how long they had been in the cave, for it had seemed like days and weeks, and yet it was plain this could not be, for their candles were not yet gone. They made their way to a small spring, and sat down before it. Nothing was said for some time. Then Becky broke the silence.

"Tom, I'm so hungry."

Tom took something out of his pocket.

"Do you remember this?"

Becky almost smiled.

"It's our wedding cake, Tom."

"I saved it from the picnic. It's all we got."

Tom divided the cake and they finished their meager feast with the cold water from the spring.

"Becky, can you bear it if I tell you something?"

Becky's face paled, but she thought she could.

"Well then, we must stay here, where there's water to drink. We're down to our last candle."

Becky gave loose to tears and wailing. Tom did what he could to comfort her, but to little effect. At length, Becky said:

"Tom?"

"Well?"

"They'll miss us and hunt for us!"

"Yes, they certainly will."

"Maybe they're hunting for us now."

"Well, I reckon they are. I hope they are."

A frightened look on Becky's face made him realize their blunder. Becky was not to have gone home that night! They both realized that Sunday would be half over before Mrs. Thatcher discovered that Becky was not at Mrs. Harper's. The children fastened their eyes on the last bit of candle and watched it melt slowly and pitilessly away. The feeble flame finally rose up, lingered a moment, and then—the horror of the darkness engulfed them.

After what seemed like a mighty stretch of time, both awoke out of a deep stupor of sleep and resumed their miseries once more. Tom tried to get Becky to talk, but her sorrows were too oppressive, and all of her hopes were gone. The hours wasted away and hunger came to torment the captives again. For a while, they fancied they heard far-off shouting—rescuers—but they could not move effectively in the smothering darkness, and shortly the distant shoutings faded and were gone altogether.

They groped their way back to the spring. Time dragged on; they slept again, and this time when they awoke, Becky had given up her last vestiges of hope and could barely bring herself to speak.

Tom was struck with a desperate idea. He took a kite line from his pocket, tied it to a projection, and he groped ahead in the darkness, alone, unwinding the kite string as he progressed. At the end of forty or fifty feet, the corridor ended and several others began. Tom picked an avenue and began to unwind the kite string still farther, when, far off in the darkness, a human hand, holding a candle, appeared from behind a rock. Tom lifted a glorious shout, and instantly that hand was followed by the body it belonged to— Injun Joe. Joe's clothing was tattered and filthy, covered in blood and muck, as was his face, but he seemed remarkably hale. Tom was vastly relieved to see Joe take to his heels immediately and get himself out of sight. Tom followed the kite string back and retreated from the area, and he told himself he would return to the spring and stay there, not wishing to run the risk of meeting Joe again. He did not tell Becky what it was he had seen.

They slept again, and woke even more wretched than before. Tom believed it had been five or six days, and that the search for them had been by now abandoned. He proposed to explore another passageway. Becky was very weak. She had sunk into a dreary apathy and could not be roused. She said she would wait, now, where she was—and die. She told Tom to go on with the kite string and explore, but she made him promise that when the awful time came, he would stay by her and hold her until it was all over.

Tom kissed her and made a show of being confident in finding an escape from the cave.

"My Tom," she whispered forlornly.

"Go back to sleep," he whispered back. Then he took the kite line and went groping down one of the passages on his hands and knees, distressed with weariness and hunger, and sick with the feeling of an ultimate, approaching doom.

32

Escape and Confinement

Tuesday afternoon came, and waned to the twilight. The entire village still mourned. The lost children had not been found. Public prayer had been offered up for them, and many a private prayer that had the petitioners' whole heart in them, but still no good news came from the cave. The majority of the searchers had given up the quest and gone back to their daily avocation, saying that it was plain the children would never be found. Mrs. Thatcher was very ill, and a great deal of the time delirious. People said it was heartbreaking to hear her call her child, and raise her head to listen whole minutes at a time, then lay wearily back down with a moan. Aunt Polly had drooped into a settled melancholy, and her gray hair had grown almost white. The village went to its rest on Tuesday night, sad and forlorn.

In the middle of the night, a wild peal burst from the village church bells, and in moments the streets were swarming with frantic half-clad people shouting, "They're found! They're found!" Tin pans and horns were added to the din, the population massed itself and moved toward the river, the children coming to the village in an open carriage, and the shouting citizens thronged around it, joining its homeward march, and swept magnificently up the main street roaring huzzah after huzzah.

The village was illuminated; nobody went to bed again; it was the greatest night the little town had ever known. During the first half hour a procession of villagers filed through Judge Thatcher's house, seized the saved ones and kissed them, squeezed Mrs. Thatcher's hand, and drifted raining tears all over the place.

Aunt Polly's happiness was complete, and Mrs. Thatcher's nearly so. It would be complete as soon as a messenger was dispatched with the great news to the cave, as Judge Thatcher could not bring himself to give up hope and leave. Tom lay upon a sofa and eagerly told the history of his adventure, putting in many striking additions and descriptions to adorn it withal.

He told how he left Becky at the spring and followed several avenues as far as the kite string would reach. He told how he had seen Joe and heard him speaking, presumably to his original confederate. Joe's partner was frightened, and thirsty, ready to give up and throw up his hands, marching out of the cave in exchange for a crust of bread, a cup of water, and whatever punishment they were ready to mete out. Joe wouldn't have it; he said he no longer hungered and no longer thirsted, and the blackness of the cave did nothing to frighten him. He said he was content to wait until the last searcher had given up and gone home; then he would make his way to the surface, where he would take to the woods and quickly gather together a great army of the undead. This made his confederate balk even more, so Joe finally stopped arguing and just fell upon the man, killing him quickly with his hands. Tom's terror at this point was beyond measure, and he crouched in the darkness, figuring he was going to die next.

Joe continued to speak to his murdered confederate, telling him it was the birth of a whole new world, a glorious new beginning, and that they were going to witness it together. He said he realized the attack on the widow's compound was stupid and egotistical and premature, and it was a great lesson; he would never be so stupid again. Presently, Tom heard a rustling and a second voice said:

"I wish you hadn't 'a done that."

Joe laughed. "Settle yourself down. It was time—you were way overdue. But now it's over. No more hunger. No more thirst. It's all been sloughed off. You're better than you were an hour ago."

"I suppose. I suppose."

"Then stop your sniveling! Just sit and collect yourself a minute. You'll see! And you'll be thanking me! This is just the beginning of things."

The two went off into the darkness, nearer to the mouth of the cave, to wait for the last of the searchers to disband their efforts. Tom went back to Becky and made her drink some more water from the spring, but told her nothing of the horrible scene he had just witnessed. In a while, he explored using the kite string again, and was about to turn back when he glimpsed a far-off speck that looked like daylight. He dropped the line and crawled toward it, then scrabbled forward and pushed his head and shoulders through a small hole and saw the mighty Mississippi rolling by! And if it had happened at night, he would not have seen that speck of daylight and would not have explored that passage again! He told the listeners that he went back to Becky and broke the good news, and she told him not to fret with such stuff, for she was tired, and sick, and knew she was going to die— and even wanted to. He described how he labored with her and convinced her; and how she almost died for joy when she actually saw the blue speck of daylight; how he pushed his way out of the hole and then helped her out; how they sat there and cried for gladness; how some men came along in a skiff and Tom hailed them and told them their situation and their famished condition; how the men didn't believe them at first—"because," they said, "you are five miles down the river below the valley the cave is in"—then they took them aboard, rowed to a house, gave them blankets and supper, made them rest for several hours, and then brought them home.

Their days and nights of toil and hunger in the cave were not to be shaken off at once, as Tom and Becky soon discovered. They were bedridden all Wednesday and Thursday, and they seemed to grow more tired and worn all the time.

Tom got up and was about, a little, on Thursday, and was whole as ever by Saturday. Becky, however, did not leave her room for over a week, and then looked as if she had passed through a wasting illness.

Tom learned of Huck's illness and went to see him as soon as he was able, but was not admitted to the bedroom. After several more days, he was admitted, but was warned to keep still about his adventure and introduce no exciting topic. The Widow Douglas stayed by to see that he obeyed these rules. At home, Tom learned of the thwarted attack on the widow's compound, and the subsequent defeat of Injun Joe's forces.

He stopped at the Thatcher house every day to see how Becky was doing. On the third day, the judge was there, and he asked Tom several pointed questions about his adventure, specifically about Joe and his intentions. Tom offered his opinion that Joe and his confederate were still lurking somewhere in the cave, waiting for an expeditious departure.

The judge seemed entirely satisfied with this answer. "Then he's trapped himself and anyone else he has with him. I had the main entrance sheathed with boiler iron as soon as I heard the both of you were safely out. It's bolted and locked, and I'm the only one with keys."

"So he's probably still there."

The judge nodded his head. "In a day or so, we'll get the sheriff and have him get some men together and drag him off to jail. And soon after to a noose—or whatever it takes to rid the world of him. Don't you worry, Tom. That devil is within our grasp. We won't let him escape again!"

Tom turned white as a sheet and said nothing. The idea of being anywhere within Joe's grasp was not a pleasant one. He had had enough of Joe, and the judge's grim confidence did not comfort him whatsoever.

33

Joe's Fate

By early the next morning, the news of Injun Joe's unintentional entrapment had spread throughout the village, and a large group of somber, well-armed men met at Judge Thatcher's. The sheriff arrived shortly thereafter and deputized them in a group, and told them it was his plan to bring Joe in to trial for any number of serious, hanging offenses. He had never arrested a Zum before, and to the best of his recollection, no one else had either. Still, without belaboring the situation, it seemed prudent to proceed as if they were simply on the track of a murderer who was cautious about his own mortality. He hadn't the time or the inclination to think about it further. There were lawyers to sort out the rest of it.

Soon a dozen skiffloads of these men were on their way to the cave. The ferryboat, packed with the more adventurous, soon followed. Tom was one of the few children allowed on the boat, as it was going to be an unpleasant occasion, something unsavory but necessary, and the adults were adamant on keeping their children away from it. Tom was allowed passage due to his recent notoriety, his bravery in saving Becky, and his earlier heroism at the schoolhouse.

By the time the ferryboat arrived at its destination, the men were standing in nervous groups in front of the cave. The Welshman was there with his one able-bodied son, sitting in a light carriage. In the back of this carriage sat a number of small barrels. They were all filled with whale oil, and it was his idea to merely crack them open and pour the contents down into the mouth of the cave without opening the door, then pitch in a lit kerosene lamp. It was a sensational plan that minimized risk, but the sheriff was against it. Joe hadn't been found guilty of anything—just yet—and the sheriff wasn't going to authorize so drastic a plan on Tom's story that Joe and his confederate were some kind of new Zum who could speak and plan elaborate and nefarious activities. Let it be proved in a court of law first, he said, and that was the last word on the subject. The Welshman responded that it was a grave mistake, and the sheriff said that it was his mistake to make, so in the end, the Welshman left the carriage tied to a bush and went down, armed, to join the other men.

"Hello in the cave! Hello in the cave! Can you hear us? Joe!" Judge Thatcher shouted. "We've come from town to take you to jail! This is the only exit! Come out now!" Judge Thatcher knew, as did everyone else who had heard Tom's story, that there was another exit, but he was counting on Joe hanging close to the main entrance. He was correct in his assumption. In a few minutes, a shout came from inside the mouth of the cave.

"I'm comin' out! I'm comin' out! I'm unarmed! Neither of us are armed! Lower your weapons, gents. We mean no trouble!"

Tom was at the front of the spectators, frozen to the spot. He wanted to run as he recognized Joe's voice, but could not move. He saw the Welshman standing with the men and caught his eye, shaking his head. Don't believe him! Whatever he says is a lie! The Welshman seemed to have no trouble understanding Tom, and nodded dourly back.

Seconds later, Injun Joe and his confederate exited the cave, their hands held high. They were both pale, unnaturally pale, and Joe was tinged with a little purple and green, but both seemed submissive. Still, no one moved forward to take them into custody, and this reticence was not lost on Joe.

"What do you have here? Twenty, twenty-five men to bring me in? It's an honor, surely, but hardly warranted. We neither of us have guns. We'll go quietly," said Joe.

Judge Thatcher moved forward with a length of rope to bind the first of the two, and came up to Joe's accomplice.

"Put your hands behind you. Slowly!"

He lowered his gun to bind the rope, and Joe said in a quiet voice:

"Do it now!"

His confederate lunged at Judge Thatcher with such ferocity that they were immediately in a heap on the ground.

The confederate clawed and grappled and bit, and because of their proximity, no one from the group of men dared fire their weapons. Several other men dropped their weapons completely and rushed forward to separate the two, and soon they too were on the ground, rolling around and in general unsuccessful in gaining the upper hand. Injun Joe kept his hands held high and seemed pleased by the show. His confederate got his hands around Judge Thatcher's neck and the judge let out a sudden cry of surprise and pain.

In the next moment, one of the sheriff's men moved forward and put his gun to the side of the confederate's head and fired, but it was too late. The judge's neck had been broken, his throat crushed, and he was dead. The confederate lay on his side, half of his face gone, and struggled to get to his feet, but could not. Another shot was fired into his head and he lay mostly still. The deputies who had attempted to help the judge were splattered with blood and brain matter and in obvious distress. There was a secret terror, unproven but entirely reasonable, that this kind of blood spray was one way to incubate an infestation.

"He were a handful, warn't he?" Joe asked.

The sheriff moved forward with his own gun pointed at Joe's head and responded:

"And you'll wind up just the same as him if you do the slightest thing to warrant it."

"Warrant? Me? No. I'll take my chances in a court of law. I've seen lots of things happen there to give me hope. You'll get no fight out of me."

The Welshman took out another coil of rope and moved

to bind Joe for transport to jail, but Tom cried out from the edge of the crowd:

"Stop! Don't do it! Don't believe a word! I seen him kill his pal and raise him up again! He means to get an army of undead and kill us all. Oh, please . . ."

Joe looked at Tom and smiled pleasantly. "You're the boy from the trial, ain't you? Always stickin' your young nose where it don't belong. Well, I won't do anything about it right now, but these habits of yours are going to—"

An explosion interrupted Joe's casual threat, coming from the Welshman's gun. His shot tore into Joe's knees, knocking him off his feet. Joe seemed mildly surprised. "This is a fine way to treat an unarmed prisoner."

The Welshman responded: "I've had enough of you, Joe. You've done harm to my son, too. You may be a hard man to kill, but you're not so hard to bring down." He lifted his fowling shotgun and shot him again in the legs.

Joe supported himself with his arms and began cursing at the Welshman. "I demand me a trial! In a court of law!"

The sheriff moved forward with his own fowling piece and shot Joe once in the face with a terrific blast. Joe flew back onto the dirt and moved sporadically.

"Drag the judge's body out of there and bring me some of that whale oil," he told whoever was listening to him.

Two barrels of the whale oil were unloaded and the judge's body put into that space in back of the carriage. Tom had moved forward out of a morbid curiosity, and Joe began slithering toward him on his hands. "You!" he hissed.

The Welshman stood in front of Tom and looked him in

the eyes with a gaze of utter sadness and remorse. "I'm sorry you're here to see all this," he said. Then he poured a combination of the whale oil and kerosene over Joe's un-dead body and lit it with a lucifer match. The crowd from the ferryboat moved back in quiet horror as Joe continued to struggle, beyond pain and the words to express it. In a while, the flames gathered intensity, the smoke rose black and acrid, and his struggles stopped.

The pyre of Injun Joe lasted the entire day, and when the fire at last burned itself out, he was shoveled apart into smaller pieces, and buried at the spot. For years afterward, people flocked there in boats and wagons from the towns and farms for miles around; they brought their children, and all sorts of provisions, and confessed that they had had a much better time than had they actually been to the event. Joe was responsible for the killing of at least five citizens of the village, but everyone knew it could have been much worse. He was a new type of Zum that had never been seen before, one that commanded other Zum and made them do his bidding. It would have been a major calamity had he had the opportunity to gather a dozen like souls. Had he gath-ered a hundred or two—it was something that no one could even bring themselves to think about.

Judge Thatcher had a large and well-attended funeral. Mrs. Thatcher had been with him for the majority of a life-time, and wore black for a year afterward. Becky wore black too, and remained in her house for more than a week, mostly attending to her mother, making her tea and cups of warmed broth.

Several mornings after the funeral, Tom took Huck to a private place to have an important talk. Huck had learned all about the adventure from the Welshman and the Widow Douglas, but Tom reckoned there was one thing they had not told him. Huck's face saddened, and he said:

"I know what it is. You got into Number Two and never found anything but whiskey. Nobody told me, but I figured it out—I figured if you'd found the money you'd'a get to me one way or the other." Then Huck told Tom his entire adventure, starting with his stalking Injun Joe and his confederate from the alley. Tom had only heard the Welshman's version of it before.

"Well," said Huck, presently coming back to the question at hand, "whoever nipped the whiskey in Number Two nipped the money, too, I reckon—anyways it's a goner for us, Tom."

"Huck, that money never was in Number Two!"

"What?" Huck searched his comrade's face. "Tom, have you got on the track of that money again?"

"Huck, it's in the cave!"

Huck's eyes blazed.

"Say it again, Tom."

"The money's in the cave."

"In earnest?"

"In earnest, Huck. Will you go back in there with me and help get it out?"

"You bet I will! I will if there's a way we get in there and not get lost."

"Huck, we can do that without the least little bit of trouble in the world."

"All right then—it's a deal! When do you say?"

"Right now, if you're strong enough."

"Is it far into the cave? I've been on my back awhile, and I've only been walkin' around for two or three days now. I don't think I could walk more'n a mile or so."

"I can take you right to it in a skiff. I can float the skiff myself, and I'll pull it back again too. It won't be too bad."

"Then let's go."

A trifle after noon the boys borrowed a small skiff from a citizen who was absent, and got under way at once. When they were several miles from the cave, Tom said:

"See that white place up yonder where it looks like there's been a landslide? Well, that's one of my marks. We'll get ashore, now."

They landed the skiff and anchored it in the mud.

"Now, Huck, where we're a-standing, you could touch that hole I got out of with a fishing pole. See if you can find it."

Huck searched all over and found nothing. Tom proudly marched into a thick clump of sumac bushes and said:

"Here you are! Look at it, Huck—it's the snuggest little hole in the country. You just keep mum about it."

Huck agreed, and the boys crawled into the hole, Tom in the lead. When they made their way into a larger area, both stood and Tom lit two creosote torches for illumination. The torches sputtered and gave off a dense and foul smoke, but the boys didn't care, as they didn't intend to stay too long. Together, they toiled down the tunnel, leaving a trail of secure kite string. A few more turns brought them to the spring where Becky had completely lost hope, and Tom felt a shudder quiver all through him. He wasn't fond of the place. They went on and on, presently entering another corridor. Tom whispered:

"Now I'll show you something, Huck." He held his candle aloft and said:

"Do you see that? There—on the big rock over yonder—done with candle smoke."

"Why, Tom, it's a cross!" He stared at the symbol for a while, then said with a shaky voice:

"Tom, let's git out of here!"

"What! And leave the treasure?"

"Yes—leave it. Injun Joe's ghost is round there, certain."

"No it ain't, Huck. It would haunt the place where he died, and that would have been the tavern. Or he'd haunt the place where he was brought down—away at the mouth of the cave—and that would be five miles from here!"

"Tom, I didn't think of that. I reckon we should climb down and have a hunt for that box."

They searched the floor of the whole area, and presently Tom struck something with his Barlow, just a few inches from the surface.

"Hey, Huck—you hear that?"

They both began to dig. It was the treasure box, sure enough.

"Got it at last!" said Huck, plowing among the tarnished coins with his hands. "My, but we're rich, Tom!"

"I always reckoned we'd get it. Say—let's not fool around here. Let's haul it out. Lemme see if I can lift the box."

Suddenly, they heard an odd gurgling cough echoing through the cave and both boys froze. They waved their torches around and saw nothing but the flicker of light reflecting from the rock walls. Again they heard the same gurgling moan, and realized they were not alone. Somewhere in the cave wandered at least one more Zum.

Tom pulled at the treasure box. It weighed about fifty pounds. He could lift one end of it, after an awkward fashion, but it was going to be hard to carry the thing out and not have to abandon their torches in the process.

"Maybe it's best to leave it here and come back at a better time," Huck whispered, but they both knew there would never be a good time, nor a better time. For Tom, coming back to the place a third time would almost be an impossibility. It would have to be now.

Huck wedged his torch between a few loose rocks and hauled the box completely out of its hiding place. "This might not be so bad," he began in feigned cheerfulness, just as Tom cried out.

"Huck! Look out!"

A Zum stumbled out of the darkness, and Huck recognized him as one of Injun Joe's men from the attack at the widow's compound. He had been shot in the back of the head, and although he had come back, it had not been as one of Joe's new order. He could not speak and seemed to have trouble moving. But it was a Zum all right.

Huck dropped the treasure box and lunged away from the creature, who was all clawing, grasping hands. This left Tom with the only torch, and Huck seemed to disappear into the blackness.

"Huck!"

"Tom! I'm behind you! See if you can back him up a foot or two and I'll make a grab for the torch. Forget the treasure. Let's just make it out of here!"

Tom waved his torch in front of the Zum, but instead of making it retreat, the flames infuriated it and it lurched forward, and with a wild wave of its hands, knocked the remaining torch out of Tom's grasp. It flew several feet and hit the wall, sending up sparks and a brief, brilliant flare of light.

The Zum continued to move forward. In the confines of the cave, it was almost a clever move, as the boys had few places to retreat to. Tom ran over to his torch, picked it up, and was met immediately by the Zum. Even in the miserable light, Tom could see that the bullet had passed completely through the front of his head. The horror of it froze him for a second, and in that moment, the Zum was upon him.

"Hold on, Tom!" Huck cried, and swung his torch at what was left of the Zum head. The contact set off yet another brief explosion of creosote and the creature released Tom to face his new attacker. Huck swung again and hit the Zum in mid-chest. This time, the creosote began to burn into the creature's ruined clothing.

By now, both boys' eyes were burning, and the smoke from the torches made it almost impossible for them to see.

Still, Tom found his own torch and brought it down on the Zum's back, making it lose its balance and stagger forward. Huck moved aside as the Zum stumbled by him and thus avoided contact with the creature. The remnants of the Zum's shirt began smoking, and in another instant, the creature was covered with small, lapping tongues of flame. It began to make a sound that was close to a wet scream.

The Zum turned and charged. It screamed as it drove past Tom, into a small corridor that neither boy had explored. There, it stumbled off a narrow, gravelly ledge and fell into a small pit about fifteen feet deep. The flames continued lapping at the Zum, who could no longer get to his feet, and Huck threw his own torch into the pit, hoping to accelerate the flames.

They stared at the wretched creature for only a few seconds, until Huck remembered: "The treasure! How hard can it be?" And so the boys brought the money to the surface, resting briefly in exhaustion by the sumac bushes next to the hole. As the sun dipped toward the horizon, they pushed out in their weighted skiff and got under way. They landed shortly after dark.

"Now, Huck," said Tom, "we'll hide the money outside the Welshman's compound, and we'll come back in the morning to count it and divide it."

When the boys reached the Welshman's compound with the heavy box, they stopped again to rest. Almost immediately, the Welshman came out and said:

"Hello, who's that?"

"Huck, and Tom Sawyer."

"Good! Come along with me, boys, you're keeping everyone waiting. Here—hurry up, trot ahead—I'll carry this thing for you. Why, it's not as light as it might be. Got bricks in it?

"Old metal," said Tom.

"Ah well, old metal then. In any case, hurry along, hurry along!"

The boys wanted to know what the hurry was about.

"Never mind; you'll see, when we get to the Widow Douglas's."

Huck said with some apprehension—for he was long used to being falsely accused:

"Mr. Jones, we haven't been doing anything."

The Welshman laughed.

"I wouldn't know about that, my boy."

They approached the widow's compound, and the Welshman called out to one of the many guards, and they opened the main door. They left the heavy box on the inside of the front door and proceeded to a grand drawing room. It was marvelously lighted, and everyone that was of any consequence in the village was there. The widow came up to receive them.

"Come with me, boys," she said. She took them to a bedchamber and said: "Now wash and dress yourselves. There's two new suits of clothes, shirts, socks, everything complete. One for you and one for Tom. Get into them. We'll wait—come down when you are slicked up enough."

She smiled briefly at them both, then closed the door and left.

34

The Big Surprise

Huck said: "Tom, we can git out of here if we can find a rope. The window ain't that far from the ground."

"Shucks, what do you want to leave for?"

"Well, I ain't used to that kind of crowd. I can't stand it."

"Oh, it ain't anything. I don't mind it a bit. I'll take care of you."

Sid appeared at the door.

"Tom," he said, "Auntie has been waiting for you all afternoon. Mary got your Sunday clothes ready, and everyone downstairs is ready."

"What's this blow-up all about, Siddy?" Tom asked.

"It's one of the widow's get-togethers that she's always having. This time it's for the Welshman and his sons, on account of that scrape they helped her out with the other night. And on account of the Welshman's son, who got whacked pretty hard—he ain't here, but it seems he's going to be all right. There's some other surprises, too."

Some while later everyone was at the supper table downstairs, and at the proper time, the Welshman made his little speech. He thanked the widow for the honor she was doing both himself and his sons, but said that there was another person present whose modesty prevents . . .

And so on and so on. He sprung his secret about Huck's share in the adventure in the finest dramatic manner he could muster. The widow made so many compliments and lay so much gratitude upon Huck that he almost forgot the nearly intolerable discomfort of his new clothes. She finished by saying she wanted to give Huck a home under her roof and have him educated; and that when she could spare the money she would start him in business in a modest way. Tom saw his chance, and said:

"Huck don't need it. He's already rich."

It was a pleasant, odd joke that no one knew quite how to take, so the silence that followed was a little awkward. Tom broke it himself:

"Huck's got plenty of money. Maybe none of you believe, but it's true. I reckon I can show you a thing. Just wait a minute."

Tom ran to the front door to retrieve the heavy box. Soon, he reentered the room, dragging it across the floor, struggling with the weight of it. He opened the box, poured a handful of gold coins upon the dining room table and said:

"There—what did I tell you? Half of it's Huck's and half of it is mine!"

The spectacle of the pile of gold took everyone's breath away. All gazed, and no one could find the words to begin speaking. Then everyone began to have the same thoughts at once, and there was a unanimous call for an explanation. Tom said he could furnish it, and he did. The tale was long, but the room was rapt and silent. There was scarcely an interruption from anyone to break the charm of the story. When he had finished, the money was counted. The sum amounted to a little over twelve thousand dollars. It was more than anyone had ever seen at one time before, though several people who were there were worth considerably more than that in property.

35

Plans

The reader may rest assured that Tom and Huck made quite a nice stir in the little village. So vast a sum, all in gold (with some silver pieces here and there) seemed next to incredible. It was talked about, gloated over, until many of the good citizens teetered under the strain of a very unhealthy excitement. Every "haunted" house for miles around was dissembled, plank by plank, and its foundation dug up and ransacked for hidden treasure—and not by boys, but by men. Wherever Tom and Huck appeared, they were courted, admired, and stared at. Everything they did seemed to be something regarded as remarkable. Their past history was raked up and discovered to bear marks of conspicuous originality. The village paper published biographical sketches of the boys, including a fine ink drawing of Tom and Huck, standing proudly on the rotting corpse of an angry Zum.

The Widow Douglas put their money out at six percent. Each lad had an income, now, that was simply prodigious—a dollar for every weekday in the year, and half of the Sundays. That much money could board, lodge, and school a boy in those days—and clothe him and arm him, for that matter.

The Widow Thatcher had conceived a great opinion of Tom. She said that no one else could have gotten her daughter out of that cave—and this included her late husband, who had headed the unsuccessful rescue efforts for the two. When Becky told her mother that Tom had taken her whipping for her at school, the woman was visibly moved. She began to look at Tom as a part of their family, and she utterly approved of Tom and her daughter as a fine and noble couple—two people who were perfect for each other.

Huck Finn remained at the Widow Douglas's for less than a month, then one day turned up missing. For forty-eight hours the widow looked for him everywhere in great distress. Early on the third day, Tom Sawyer went wisely poking among some old barrels behind the deserted slaughterhouse, and found Huck there. He was unkempt, uncombed, and clad in the same old rags that made him picturesque when he was free and happy. Tom routed him out, told him the trouble he was causing, and urged him to go home. Huck's face lost its tranquil content and took on a melancholy cast. He said:

"It ain't for me, Tom. The widder's good to me, but I can't stand their ways. The widder eats by a bell, she goes to sleep by a bell—everything's so awful a body can't hardly stand it. Awful! I got to ask to go fishin', I got to ask to go swimmin'. Widder wouldn't let me smoke, or yell, or scratch myself good in front of folks. And dad fetch it, she prayed all the time! I had to leave, Tom, I just had to. Looky-here, Tom, be- ing rich ain't what it's cracked up to be. I wish I was dead most of the time. Tell you what—you just take my share of the money. I don't want it no more. No, Tom, I won't be rich, and I won't live in them cussed smothery houses!"

Tom saw his opportunity and replied:

"Look here, Huck, the money's yours to do with what you like. So what *would* you like to do with it?"

Huck brightened up somewhat. "Oh, that's easy. I liked bein' a pirate, and I liked playin' robber, but you know what I had the best time at?"

"What's that?" asked Tom.

"Huntin' those durn Zum. Trackin' 'em, trailin' 'em, bringin' 'em to ground! I know Joe was a frightful, terrible thing, but he deserved everything he got, and I liked that I had a hand in it. I could do that ag'in and ag'in. We got the money—heck, we could go from town to town and help people take a stand against the Zum! Even if they was as bad as Injun Joe, or worse! We could put together a real gang—a regular crew—and I know for certain the Welsh- man's one son would go for it in the twinklin' of an eye, soon as he's healed up. He's got no love for the undead— 'specially now that they seem to be gettin' smarter. Oh, I don't know."

Tom was silent for some time. Finally, he said:

"It would take awhile to put together proper. But, heck, we got the money—why *shouldn't* we be able to take a crack at it?"

"Now you're talkin', Tom."

"Tell you what. You go back to the widow for just a while longer, whilst I put this thing together. I'll have the widow draw the money for us and start putting together a plan. And I'll ask her to let up on you a little, Huck."

"Will you, Tom—now will you? That's good. If she'll let up a bit, I'll smoke private and cuss private, long as I know there's some kind of end in sight. When you fix on startin' to put together the plan?"

"Oh, right off. Truth is, I already been thinking about something mighty similar. Seems like goin' up against the Zum would be the best idea—a little bit pirate, a little bit Robin Hood. Everyone in town would be real proud of us. Becky says if that's what I got a mind to do, she's all for it— seein' how they kilt the judge—as long as I promise to come back in one piece, which I plan to do. We'll have ourselves a real gang, one that people will be happy to see, and we could have some kind of initiation to join."

"Some kind of what?"

"Initiation," Tom explained. "It's to swear to stand by one another—all of us—and never show fear, or betray each other's secrets, even if the Zum have you up against it and are tryin' to chop you up into little pieces, and kill anyone that hurts one of the gang."

"That sounds mighty fine, Tom. Mighty fine."

"And you've got to swear on a coffin—one that has a Zum bangin' on from the insides—and sign the oath in blood."

"Why, Tom, that's a million times better than piratin'! I'll go back to the widder's till I rot, long as I know we're going to be doin' something this fine. And if we get to be really famous, bringin' down Zum, and everyone talkin' about it, I reckon the widder'll be proud she took me out of the wet and brought me into her house. Polly, too. Oh Tom, this is the best idea ever!"

And they spat on their palms and put their hands to it.

CONCLUSION

Thus ends the chronicle of Tom's first adventures with the undead. It being strictly the history of a boy, it must stop here; the story could not go much farther without it being the history of a man. When one writes of juveniles, one must stop where he best can.

Most of the characters in this book still live, though not all. Most are prosperous and happy. Some day it may seem worthwhile to take up the story again and see what sort of men and women they turned out to be. The world is changing, to be sure. The Zum seem to have evolved, becoming something they hadn't been before. The people, however, are changing too. Hardship and misfortune can do that to a people. Therefore it will be wisest not to reveal any more of their lives at present.

TOR

Award-winning authors
Compelling stories

Please join us at the website
below for more information
about this author and other great
Tor selections, and to sign up for
our monthly newsletter!